GUNS HAD RULED HIS LIFE . . .

They'd bought him power and even a twisted kind of fame—but they'd also cost him eleven years. Eleven years of being whipped regularly, three times a month, in a stinking hole of a prison camp. Parker was older now, wiser, and he'd vowed never to tote a gun again.

But as he stared down at the cold body in the dust, something began to pull at his guts. The dead man had been a gunslinger, a killer. He had also been just about the only man Sam Parker could call a friend. Parker hesitated for a moment —then he bent down and took the Colt revolver from the lifeless hand . . .

THE DAWN RIDERS

THE DAWN RIDERS

Frank Gruber

BANTAM BOOKS
Toronto • New York • London • Sydney

THE DAWN RIDERS
A Bantam Book / October 1968

PRINTING HISTORY
New Bantam edition / May 1977
2nd printing . . . September 1982

ISBN 0-553-22679-7

Published simultaneously in the United States and Canada

Bantam Books are published by Bantam Books, Inc. Its trade-
mark, consisting of the words "Bantam Books" and the por-
trayal of a rooster, is Registered in U.S. Patent and Trademark
Office and in other countries. Marca Registrada. Bantam
Books, Inc., 666 Fifth Avenue, New York, New York 10103.

PRINTED IN THE UNITED STATES OF AMERICA

H   11 10 9 8 7 6 5 4 3 2

THE DAWN RIDERS

During the day the piney woods sweltered, even though the sun touched the soggy earth only in patches here and there. In the night a miasmic mist fell upon the turpentine woods. It was always heaviest among the cluster of buildings that were the prison camp.

Mortality was heavy among the prisoners. Some went mad during their first month, others succumbed from disease, malnutrition, or in desperate, futile escape attempts. Not more than twenty per cent of the chain gang lasted a year, but there was never a shortage of men. Fresh ones were recruited continuously, from the state penitentiary, from the county jails.

No one knew how long Sam Parker had been in the camp for there was also a large turnover of guards and overseers. Some sickened, some died. Most of them merely quit their jobs, preferring to eke out a more miserable existence away from the piney woods.

Sam Parker was the oldest prisoner, in point of longevity. He was also the worst incorrigible in Camp Number Three. He was lashed on an average of three times a month and in between received a few blows of the fist and sometimes a smashing blow with the butt of a rifle.

Parker was nasty. He was mean and he was cruel.

1

twenty men to a shack, ten on each side. Each man wore shackles and when they were herded into a shack a chain was run through a large ring in the middle of the shackle chain. Ten men, on each side, were fastened to one another, so that at night escape was impossible for an individual. If all were loosened all could escape, but if none were freed of the chain none could escape.

It was just as well, for no escapee could exist in the piney woods. Not without food, not without a gun. Not with twenty bloodhounds baying them down, tearing them to pieces.

It had been a bad day. The temperature had been at a record high. One man had died shortly after noon, seven had collapsed from the heat. Others had shirked their work and the prison contractor would be dissatisfied with the day's production.

The bread was moldy, there were maggots in the salt beef. The water was tepid and there was life in it. A new prisoner sobbed openly. None of the others in the shack paid any attention. Misery is a personal thing.

Parker, at the far end of the right hand line of prisoners, knew that Bucko Smith, the overseer, would be paying a visit that evening.

He was right. Bucko came into the shack and with him were two guards instead of the customary one.

He stood just inside the shack, teetering lightly back and forth on the balls of his feet.

"Well, gentlemen," he said after awhile, "it's nice to see you taking your evening's rest after a good day's work. An honest day's work." He prodded with his toe the man nearest to him. "Eh, Bucko?"

The prisoner was an older man and knew better than to reply. Bucko Smith grinned wolfishly. "You *did* give me an honest day's work, didn't you?" He shook out the coiled blacksnake whip. "I'm talking to you, Bucko!"

The blacksnake lashed the air, crackled as it bit into the prisoner's skin. It snapped again and again. Five lashes.

The two guards took the left hand line, singling out a man here and there for three lashes or five—ten to one of the men who had wasted an hour by fainting.

Bucko, on his side, gave no man less than five lashes and three of them received ten. He skipped only one man of the first nine, then came to Sam Parker.

"Ah, Mr. Parker," he said with huge relish as he stood over the toughest man in Prison Camp Number Three. "And how are *you* this fine evening?"

"Get it over with, Bucko," snapped Parker.

"Ten lashes? Or are you trying for twenty tonight?"

"Twenty and I don't work tomorrow," retorted Parker. "Suit yourself."

Bucko Smith shook his head admiringly. "You never weaken, do you, Parker?"

"Would if make any difference if I did?"

"No, you'd get just as many lashes. And maybe a little more muscle behind them. Well, I've got a surprise for you tonight. A real surprise." He chuckled hugely. "You'll never guess, Mr. Parker, not in a year of Tuesdays."

Parker said evenly, "Thirty lashes?"

The two guards, finished with their lashings, came up behind Bucko Smith. They grinned oafishly. "There's a man, boys," chortled Bucko Smith. "He'd take thirty lashes and think nothing of it."

"Oh, I'd think about it, Bucko. I'd think about it."

3

"Well, *think* then, Parker, because it isn't thirty lashes I'm giving you tonight."

"Sooner or later you've got to kill me," Parker said tonelessly.

Smoldering regret showed in the overseer's red-lidded eyes. "No, Parker, I'm not going to kill you. I thought I would in the end, but you've licked me. I tried my best to break you, but you were too tough for me. You're free."

It was a trick, of course. Parker would be free only when he died.

He waited for the lash.

Bucko Smith said, "There's got to be an end to everything and your time's up."

The chain was removed and after awhile Parker was in the blacksmith's shop and the smith was removing the shackles from about his ankles. Still later, a moth-eaten suit was thrust at him and he was handed a burlap-wrapped bundle in which there was a chunk of ham and a heel of moldy bread.

"Thirty miles," Bucko Smith told him. "Maybe thirty-five. Straight north. There's a railroad and a depot. Ride the train or walk, but keep moving."

"And the dogs?" asked Parker.

"You still can't believe it, can you?"

"I believe in the whip," said Parker. "The whip and the rifle. And that's about all. I've been here a long time."

"How long, Parker? How long *have* you been here?"

"If I knew," said Sam Parker, "I wouldn't tell you."

Bucko Smith nodded amiably. "That's the way I'll remember you. You never whined. You never begged. There was a man over in Camp Number Seven a lot like you. He was just as tough as you, but one day he stuck a piney wood sliver through his throat. I thought *you'd* go like that sometime, but you didn't. You beat us, Parker."

Chapter Two

Freedom.

Sweet potatoes, dug from a field. Green corn, torn from the stalks. A chicken, stolen from a henhouse. A 'possum and persimmons, for a feast.

Freedom was work, back-breaking work in a lumber yard. But work without whippings. And there was money. Not much, but it *was* money with which you could buy things.

And then one day, in the city by the river, Parker saw a calendar in the window of a store. A calendar which bore the year 1874. The day—May 2nd.

May 2nd.

Deep, deep within, memory tugged at him. A date May 2, 1837. It meant something to Sam Parker.

He walked on and after a few minutes it came to him. His birth date. May 2, 1837. If May 2, 1874 was today's date, then this was his thirty-seventh birthday.

It couldn't be. He had been only twenty-six when . . .

Eleven years!

Eleven years ago. 1863 . . .

He looked around and, standing with his back to the window, watched the passers-by on the street. There were men, women, children. Men in rough clothes, men in Prince Alberts, sack suits.

Not one man in uniform.

In the distance a steamboat whistle blew. Parker

turned toward the river and after awhile found himself standing at a gangplank watching bales of cotton being loaded onto the deck of a steamer.

A purser eyed him with a jaundiced eye.

"You go to St. Louis?" Parker asked.

"Five dollars. Deck passage."

"Deck passage?"

"You sleep on the deck."

The steamboat whistle blasted the air and Parker took money from his pocket. He counted out five silver dollars and gave them to the purser.

He went aboard.

For two days Parker tramped the streets of St. Louis. He stood on the levee and watched the river steamers. He walked down Market Street and Olive. He paced Chouteau and Pine. He passed the Planters Hotel, where he had once stayed for three days.

A decision had to be made. The few dollars he had saved downriver were almost gone. He had to make a move. He did not know where to go. He did not know the North or the East, and he could not go West.

He could not stay in St. Louis. *That* he knew.

In the evening he sat on the veranda of the hotel on the levee and watched the moving lights of the boats on the river. When he paid for the night's lodging in the morning he would have a dollar left. He had to make the decision tonight.

He got up and stepped down from the veranda. He strolled along the levee and after awhile turned into one of the waterfront saloons. It was a mean place, catering to the stevedores and roustabouts, but there was a man at the bar who was neither.

He wore a Prince Albert that had seen service and his hat was somewhat the worse for having been stepped on, but he had a roll of greenbacks in his fist that was large enough to choke a Tennessee mule.

"My name is Jim Duke," he announced, "and I brought a herd of Longhorns up the Chisholm Trail. I'm on my way back to Texas to fetch up another herd. I'm having me a toot tonight that's got to last me awhile. I hate to drink alone and I'd take it kindly if every man in the place would step up and have a drink with Jim Duke."

A cheer went up and men who had been lurking about converged upon the bar. Whiskey was sloshed into glasses. A bottle was shoved along to where Parker was sipping at a glass of beer.

He shook his head.

"It's free," urged the bartender.

Parker shoved the bottle along to the next man.

A few feet away Jim Duke let out a roar that rattled the glasses on the back bar. His huge left hand swung a man away from him and it could be seen that the man had his fingers clenched about the roll of bills that Duke had stowed away in a pocket only a moment before.

"A pickpocket!" roared Jim Duke. "Now I've seen everything!"

He wrenched the wrist that he was gripping and the greenbacks tumbled to the floor and scattered. Duke struck at the face of the pickpocket.

The pickpocket ducked and a knife appeared in his hand.

"Mister," he said through his teeth, "you're big, but I'm going to slice you to pieces like one of your Texas steers."

He made a sudden swipe at Jim Duke and the knife slithered through the velvet collar of the Prince Albert. It went through the cloth below, as well as the vest and shirt and even Jim Duke's underwear. It did even better than that, for it cut the skin of Duke's chest.

Duke hurled the knife man away from him. His hand went under his ripped coat and came out with a tremendous revolver.

"Knife me, you slimy river rat!" he roared. "I'll nail your gizzard to your spine."

He might have done exactly that save for the fact that the pickpocket had a confederate, a hulking beetle-browed man who drew out a leather-covered blackjack and swung at big Jim Duke's gun hand. It landed just above the wrist and numbed Duke's hand so that the gun flew from his hand and skittered across the floor.

"I hate men from Texas," said the man with the blackjack. "I hate them worse when they've got a fistful of money and I haven't had a decent meal in four days."

He hit the big Texan in the face with the blackjack. Jim Duke cried out and fell back. The man with the blackjack followed through, smashing Duke again on the side of his head. Duke reeled against the bar and slid to the floor. The blackjack wielder surged forward to pound the Texan a few more times. In his eagerness he knocked into Parker at the bar and to get him out of the way slashed at him with the blackjack.

The shot-loaded weapon hit Parker in the face. Then Parker, who would have stood by even if the assailants had killed Jim Duke, got into the fray.

His fist lashed out and caught the beetle-browed man on the back of the neck, smashing him down and forward so that the man's head rammed the bar. Parker pivoted and faced the pickpocket with the knife.

"So you had to deal yourself in," the pickpocket said through his teeth. He came toward Parker, moving in a semicircle.

Parker stepped forward, lunged at the pickpocket and caught the man's knife arm. He twisted savagely. A scream of anguish was torn from the man's throat. The knife clattered to the floor.

Parker shoved the man away and kicked the knife across the room. The pickpocket's arm dangled at his side, broken. He reeled back moaning.

Duke was climbing to his feet. He looked around, saw that his attackers had been taken care of. He turned to Parker.

"I'm obliged to you, sir."

He reached out to catch hold of the bar to steady himself.

"You've been cut," said Parker.

"A scratch, that's all," declared Duke. He was suddenly sober, however. "If you'll be so good as to walk to the hotel with me . . ."

"I'll get you a cab," said Parker.

He turned and headed for the door. When he reached it he turned. Duke was still clinging to the bar.

"Take him with you," called the bartender.

Parker returned to the bar and took hold of Duke's arm. Leaning heavily on Parker, Duke went with him toward the door.

Outside there was no sign of a hansom cab.

"I'm staying at the Planters," said Duke. "I'd be obliged if you'd walk with me." He forced a wan smile to his lips. "I'm not in shape to take on a couple more like those two inside."

Parker had gone this far, he had to go through with it. He walked with Jim Duke to the Planters Hotel. Once or twice he almost had to lift the Texan to continue on with him and when he reached the hotel he found that it was necessary to help him up to his room on the third floor.

A doctor was summoned and while they waited for him Parker helped Duke remove his coat, shirt and undershirt. All were soaked with blood.

The knife cut was revealed then. It was not a serious wound, but it was deep enough and long enough to have caused Duke to lose much blood.

There was a knock on the door. It was the hotel physician.

He looked at the wound and shook his head. "I'm going to have to do a little needle work."

"You won't need me," said Parker then. "Good night."

"Wait!" cried Duke. "I want to talk to you." He grinned wanly. "As soon as I get sewed together."

A half hour later the doctor gave Jim Duke a sedative. "You'll be a little stiff for a few days, but in a week you'll be as good as new. I'll take out the stitches then."

"Can't wait a week," exclaimed Duke. "I've got to start for home tomorrow."

"You'll be in no condition to travel tomorrow."

Duke smiled. "I've been cut up worse'n this, Doc.

Why, during the war—" He caught himself. "Sorry, I forgot. I'm up North now."

The doctor chuckled. "I wasn't under the impression that you were a Yank, sir."

"Sixteenth Texas Cavalry."

"Seventh Missouri," replied the doctor.

"I don't believe we ever had the pleasure of opposing you."

"It wouldn't have been a pleasure," said the doctor. "It never was." He shook his head. "You'll be traveling downriver?"

"To New Orleans, yes. Then to Galveston."

"The *River Queen* has a ship's doctor. But it doesn't leave until the day after tomorrow. If you could change to the *Queen* it might be all right for you to travel."

"I'll do that."

"Very well, sir. I'll look in on you tomorrow morning."

The doctor took his leave and Jim Duke then studied Parker. "I'm greatly beholden to you, Mister . . . ?"

"Parker."

"Parker. I won't insult you by offering to pay you, but if there is anything I can do for you . . ."

"There's nothing."

"I can't let you go just like that," insisted Duke. "You live in St. Louis?"

"At the moment, yes."

Duke caught upon that. "You have no employment then?"

"I've been looking for work. I'll probably find something."

"And if you don't?"

"I may go downriver."

"Go with me. I'd be delighted to have your company. Look, Parker, I'll take the old bull by the horns. I usually do and that's how I get into trouble. The clothes you're wearing, your, ah, general appearance— you're broke?"

"I've been broke before."

"You're looking for work. Does it make any difference *where* you work?" Parker did not reply immediately and Duke broke in, "How about Texas?"

"Texas would be all right."

"Then come to Texas with me?"

"Mister," said Parker bluntly, "I helped you at the saloon only because one of those men happened to hit me. If he hadn't I wouldn't have lifted a finger to help."

Duke nodded and smiled. "Perhaps not." He suddenly yawned. "I'm too sleepy to argue now. Think it over. In any case, come and have breakfast with me. That's the least I can do for you."

Parker took leave of the Texan.

Outside he walked back to his cheap hotel on the riverfront but it was too hot and sticky to go to his room. He stood outside the hotel for awhile, then sat down in one of the veranda rocking chairs.

Chapter Three

There were lights on the river as boats moved about and there were many lights on the far shore, in Illinois. They began to go out gradually as the occupants of the houses went to bed.

After awhile Parker picked up a battered magazine that lay on the vacant chair beside him. He turned the pages idly, then was suddenly caught by an article with glaring headlines:

THE BLOODIEST ACT
OF THE WAR

Smaller headlines amplified the title:

Bloody Bill Quade Sacks Weber, Kansas
Murders 120 Unarmed Men

There was an artist's drawing of a man with lurid identification underneath: *The bloodiest man of the century. The most hated man of the war. The scourge of the border.*

Parker read the article. It was a gory account of the infamous guerrilla, Bloody Bill Quade, who with a hundred men kept twenty thousand Union troops occupied during the early years of the war, culminating with the massacre of the helpless male residents of Weber, Kansas.

The last bloody act of Quade's guerrillas had been committed in August, 1863. The band had apparently dispersed or gone into hiding after that event, but the writer of the article claimed to have inside information about the fate of Quade, obtained from secret sources—guerrillas who rode with Quade.

One of the informants, averred the writer, insisted that Quade had been killed at the battle of Westport in October, 1864. The dried ears of six men were strung on his bridle reins.

Another informant, however, denied that Quade had met his end in Missouri. He claimed to have been with Bloody Bill in Kentucky as late as July, 1865. Quade, with a remnant of his band, had gone there late in 1864, had found the area suitable to his type of operation and had spread terror and desolation in the Kentucky hills.

A large Union guerrilla force had finally been recruited to destroy Quade and the guerrilla leader had been mortally wounded in a bloody engagement. Taken to a hospital by the informant himself, Quade had passed away after lingering between life and death for more than a week. He had been buried in Kentucky under another name.

Parker's eyes returned to the portrait of Bloody Bill Quade. It was not a picture of Bill Quade and yet there were resemblances. The artist could once have seen Quade, or—a person who had seen him once could recall his features by studying this artist's conception.

Bloody Bill Quade was still remembered. He was still as hated as during the years when his name had chilled the hearts of those living in Missouri and Kansas.

There were people living who would recognize Bill Quade. No matter how much he had changed in the eleven years since the Weber Massacre, no matter what name he carried today, there were those who would know him on sight.

Parker slept fitfully that night. Before dawn he was up and seated on the rocking chair of the river hotel veranda. Finally, at seven o'clock, he walked to the Planters Hotel.

Jim Duke was still in bed. His face was drawn, he was feverish, but he was glad to see Parker.

"If you don't mind," he said, "we'll have breakfast brought up. I'm going to take it easy today so I'll be in shape to travel tomorrow." He gave Parker a quick look. "You're coming with me?"

"Yes," said Parker, "if you still want me after I tell you my real name."

Duke threw up his right hand, palm outwards. "You don't tell me anything you don't want to tell. Not now or any other time. Your personal life is your own."

He pointed to a small carpetbag on a stand nearby. "There's some money in there. Help yourself and buy some clothes." He chuckled. "They're raising cotton again down South and there's usually a few planters on the riverboats. Sometimes they take their wives with them. Or daughters."

Parker shook his head. "I'd just as soon wear what I've got."

Duke exclaimed. "Hell, man, I'm not offering you charity. An advance against your wages."

"How much will my pay be?"

Duke shrugged. "You name it."

Parker hesitated. "I don't even know what work I'll be doing. I gathered that you have a ranch."

"Yes," said Duke, "I own a ranch. The Duke Ranch." He looked sharply at Parker. "You haven't heard of it?"

Parker shook his head.

"Ah, you Northerners!" laughed Duke. He pointed again at the carpetbag. "Go ahead, open it up."

Parker stepped to the carpetbag, opened it. The bag was crammed with packets of bills. All of the bills seemed to be hundred dollar government notes.

"How much would you guess is in that bag?" asked Duke.

"I don't know—a lot."

"I sold fifty-two hundred steers in Dodge City, Kansas, for an average price of twenty-two dollars per steer. There's something over a hundred thousand dollars in that bag. I figure on sending three, maybe four herds up the trail this year." He nodded. "My pappy went down to Texas to help Sam Houston back in '36. He stayed on and took up a little land, then a little more and more and first thing he knew he had a pretty fair-sized ranch." He paused. "About a million acres. A lot of our people joined up during the war and there wasn't anybody to pay any attention to the cattle. The herds ran wild and by the time the war was over nobody knew who owned what. It didn't matter 'cause they weren't worth much anyway. Oh, a few people skinned some down and got a dollar for the hides and a little for the tallow, but you had to haul the skins and tallow to New Orleans and it was hardly worth it. Then along about '67 or '68, some fellows came down from Kansas and asked would we drive cattle up there. They had a market for beef and would pay cash on the barrel. Just happened there was an awful lot of beef feeding on our grass and we had two-three hundred people we were taking care of, so we rounded up a lot of stuff and sent it north. We been doin' it ever since." Jim Duke paused again. "I been running the ranch alone since '71, when Old Jim kicked the gong."

Parker said evenly, "I'll work for you in Texas. But not Kansas."

Jim Duke regarded Parker thoughtfully for a moment. "That's fine, Parker, just fine. Now help yourself to some of that money and go get yourself some fancy duds."

Parker skimmed a single bill from one of the packets in the carpetbag. "I'll bring back the change."

"Change!" snorted Duke.

Parker went to a store on Market Street and bought a suit of clothing, some boots, a hat and three shirts. He returned to the Planters Hotel and deposited sixty dollars on the table beside the money-bearing carpetbag.

Duke insisted that Parker use his bathroom and

Parker bathed, shaved and put on his new clothes. When he came out of the bathroom Duke surveyed him critically.

"If you'd bought some fancier duds instead of those hand-me-downs," he declared, "you could pass for a Mississippi planter—or a riverboat gambler." He grinned. "More likely a gambler. The ones I've met had your kind of eyes." He hesitated. "You've played cards?"

"Not much since the war."

Duke threw up a hand. "There I go again—asking questions. I said I wouldn't." He pointed to a roll of bills on a nearby dresser. "You'll need some spending money on the boat. Help yourself."

"What do you pay your cowboys in Texas?" asked Parker.

"Forty a month and found," said Duke. "That's the fellas who are single. The married people—well, they get their house, whatever they need for themselves, their families and—" he shrugged, "whenever I come back with a wad of money I pass out a bunch of it." He chuckled. "Sounds like the old feudal system, eh? That's the way they're used to it, the Mexicans, that is. It ain't as bad as it sounds, though. Some of the hands are second generation. They don't know any other place than the Duke spread."

"If you don't mind," said Parker, "I'll take a month's pay in advance. Forty dollars."

"Forty dollars!" exclaimed Duke. "That's what the hands get!"

"That's what I'm going to be, a hand," said Parker.

He refused to be moved and Duke finally counted out forty dollars.

Chapter Four

Early the following morning Duke and Parker boarded the *River Queen,* one of the better riverboats. They had hardly entered the cabin they would share when a steward knocked on the door and presented a card to Duke.

"Mister Fargo asked me to give you this."

"Fargo," Duke grunted to Parker. "He can't wait to get at me. Come along and tell me what you think of him. He's supposed to be the best poker player on the Mississippi."

The boat was still tied to the dock, but the saloon was well filled and a couple of games were already in session. A lean, tubercular-looking man at one of the tables waved to Duke.

"Saw your name on the passenger list," he said. "Glad to see you again."

Duke shook hands with the gambler. "I'll tell you how glad *I* am when I get to New Orleans."

He pulled back a chair and took a seat. Then he nodded to Parker. "Parker, shake hands with Mr. Fargo."

The gambler got to his feet, shook hands with Parker, then introduced the two other men at the table. One was obviously a planter, the other possibly a business man. The planter's name was Abercrombie, the other man's Shell.

17

"Care to sit in, Mr. Parker?" asked Fargo.

Parker started to shake his head, but Duke had already pulled out a chair for him. "Get your feet wet, Parker." He grinned. "They don't get really rough until the last day." To Fargo, "Deal."

Parker took out the forty dollars he had drawn against his pay. Fargo regarded the few bills thoughtfully. "We play table stakes. Ante a dollar."

Abercrombie had about a hundred dollars before him, Shell twice that much. The gambler himself had perhaps a thousand dollars in gold. Duke brought out a fat roll containing several thousand dollars.

"I'll start with this," he announced, "but I've got plenty back of it."

Fargo shuffled the cards and dealt to Shell, then Duke, Parker and finally Abercrombie.

Parker found that he had an ace, king, two sevens and a trey. Shell passed, but Duke promptly opened the pot for five dollars. Parker put in five dollars.

"I raise ten," announced Abercrombie.

"I'll call just to sweeten the pot," said Fargo.

Shell turned down his cards.

"See your ten," said Duke, "and raise ten—and I hope you raise me back."

Parker put in twenty dollars more, which left him fourteen dollars. Abercrombie looked at his cards again, merely called Duke's bet. Fargo called.

"I'll take four cards," grinned Duke. "I just wanted to get my feet wet."

Parker decided against keeping the ace for a kicker and asked for three cards. Abercrombie took three and the gambler smiled frostily.

"I'll take two."

Duke kept his hand to which he had made a four-card draw.

"I'll wait for the power," he announced.

"Check," said Parker. He had caught a third seven, a king and a four.

Abercrombie squeezed his cards. He glanced at Parker's money, nodded. "I open for fifteen dollars."

"See the fifteen and raise fifty," said Fargo.

"My feet are wet," Duke boomed, throwing in his cards. "It's up to you, Parker."

"It's table stakes," Parker said, "I'm in for what I've put up."

"We can waive it," said Abercrombie, "this early in the game."

"It's all right with me," said Fargo.

"Me too," cried Duke, "although I'm not in this pot. Go ahead, Parker, bet if you've got it."

"All right," said Parker, "I'll call the fifty—and raise two hundred."

Abercrombie gasped. "I walked into that one!"

He squeezed his cards again, counted his money, then took out a thick wallet. "I'll just call."

"I don't know, Mr. Parker," said Fargo thoughtfully, "but I've got a hunch he's bluffing. I'll call your two hundred—and raise it another two."

The man had obviously not been drawing to a possible flush or straight. But had he already had three of a kind? Or a straight with a kicker?

If it was three of a kind he probably had a larger three than Parker.

Parker glanced at Abercrombie. The man did not ring true to him. He could be a stalking horse for Fargo, his partner.

Parker said, "I'll call. I'm four hundred and fifty light in the pot."

"Too rich for me," Abercrombie said, "beats my queens and fours." He tossed in his cards.

"I had a pair of fives going in," said Fargo. "I held an ace for a kicker. I got another one. Beat aces and fives, Mr. Parker."

"Three sevens," said Parker.

Fargo's eyes narrowed as they fixed themselves upon Parker. "You win," he said.

The steamboat whistle blasted twice and a steward came into the saloon. "All ashore that's going ashore."

There was considerable commotion in the saloon and Duke suddenly pushed back his chair. "Let's have a half hour break. Until the boat gets moving."

Parker gathered in his winnings. Fargo said, "You'll be back in a half hour?"

"Perhaps."

Parker got up and followed Duke out of the saloon. "What do you think?" asked Duke.

"You're playing against a team," said Parker. "Abercrombie and Fargo."

Duke grunted. "That's what I suspicioned. They try any funny stuff I'll nail their backbones to the saloon wall."

"Fargo carries a sleeve gun."

"Sleeve gun!" exclaimed Duke.

"I'm not going to play any more," Parker said.

Duke scowled. "Fargo took me for over ten thousand the last trip. I'm going to get it back if I have to ram that sleeve gun down his throat."

"I don't carry a gun," Parker reminded.

"I'll get you one."

"No," said Parker promptly. "I—I've an aversion to firearms."

"You?" Duke stopped as they neared the ship's railing and stared at Parker. "I would have guessed you as a man handy with a shooting iron."

"Perhaps I saw too much of guns in the war," said Parker.

"Well, I saw enough myself," declared Duke, "but I wouldn't feel I was dressed without a Colt somewhere on me."

"Take Abercrombie's seat," suggested Parker. "It'll break up their pattern. And Fargo will find it more difficult for the sleeve gun if you're next to him rather than straight across."

A slow grin came over the big cattleman's features. "Sit in for an hour, Parker. We'll bring this to a head, then maybe we can play some decent poker the rest of the trip."

Parker hesitated, then shrugged.

"I'll give you five thousand to play with," said Duke. "Maybe we can get my ten thousand—and a little interest."

Parker hesitated, then nodded. Duke took a packet of large bills from a pocket and handed them to Parker.

The visitors to the boat were still leaving and there were a few late arriving passengers still boarding the steamboat, but Parker and Duke returned to the saloon.

Fargo was dealing a hand of solitaire. Abercrombie and Shell were still away from the table.

"I'm ready to play," announced Duke, seating himself in Abercrombie's vacant chair.

Parker, watching, saw annoyance flit across the gambler's face.

"You said a half hour."

"Let's play," said Duke.

Parker took the chair Duke had previously occupied. Fargo gathered together the cards, shuffled, then pushed back his chair.

"A little stretch." He began stretching himself, moving away from his chair.

"Sit down," snapped Duke. "If you're not going to play now I may not be in the mood later."

Obviously Fargo had intended moving to another chair, but the cattleman's sudden ultimatum caused him to resume his regular seat.

"Your pleasure's mine, sir," he said stiffly.

Abercrombie suddenly appeared. "You have my chair!"

"Light was in my eyes," Duke said carelessly. He indicated the chair on his right. "Sit."

Abercrombie looked at Fargo. The gambler nodded. "Let's get the game going."

"Four-handed?" asked Abercrombie.

"Look," said Duke irritably, "I had a bad night. I'd just as soon go to my cabin and sleep the rest of the day. You want to play poker now or don't you?"

Abercrombie took the chair on Duke's right. Fargo suddenly picked up the cards and, reaching out, slapped them down in front of Abercrombie.

"I believe it was your deal when we broke up."

Abercrombie shuffled the cards thoroughly, put

them out before Parker. Parker waved away the cut. Abercrombie cut them himself and dealt swiftly, smoothly.

Parker looked at his cards. He had received a pair of queens, a pair of threes and a king.

Duke chuckled over his hand: "Poker's going up. I open for fifty."

With ill grace Fargo tossed two double eagles and an eagle into the pot. Parker counted out fifty dollars with no comment.

Abercrombie said, "Since I'm the dealer I might as well deal me a good one. Up a hundred."

"Your hundred and five," retorted Duke, counting out the money.

"Before the draw?" snapped Fargo.

"It'll be more after the draw," chuckled Duke.

Fargo hesitated, looked at his cards again, then shook his head. "I shouldn't, but. . ."

He counted out the money.

A signal had obviously gone from Fargo to Abercrombie. This was to be the hand for the killing. A quick killing. Parker looked at his cards. He had two pairs, the making of a full house. He was certain he was going to get it—and get beaten. So was Duke.

He said, "Since everybody else is raising, I might as well do it myself. The five—and two thousand."

"A pat hand," snapped Fargo.

"No—but I feel lucky," said Parker.

"So do I," said Abercrombie and brought out his thick wallet. "We broke the table stakes before, so— Mr. Duke, your five hundred, Mr. Parker's two thousand —and I raise you both two thousand, five hundred."

Fargo tossed his cards into the pot. "Too much for me."

So it was Abercrombie who was going to do it for Fargo, who could be suspected. Duke let out a roar.

"This is the kind of game I like. It's forty-five hundred up to me, eh? All right, make it an even ten thousand."

Parker, watching Fargo at the moment, saw a gleam come into the gambler's eyes. Parker knew that he had guessed correctly. He called the two raises which left him with very little cash.

Abercrombie emptied his wallet, barely making Duke's raise. "I'll just call."

"I'll play these," said Duke, which did not surprise Parker. And certainly not Abercrombie.

He said, "You, too, Mr. Parker?"

"Three," said Parker.

Abercrombie blinked, then his mouth fell open. "You stayed for that much—with a pair?"

"I feel lucky," said Parker.

Across the table Fargo exclaimed angrily, "What are you, a fool?"

Duke grabbed Fargo's right arm. "Whoa, Fargo. You're forgetting yourself. Mr. Parker is my friend."

"Let him talk for himself."

"I'll take three cards," said Parker, his eyes on the pack of cards in Abercrombie's hand. "From the top."

Duke retained his grip on Fargo's arm. "You're not in this hand, Fargo. Stay out of it."

There was a long pause, then Fargo said, "All right. Play."

Abercrombie dealt three cards to Parker, hesitated, then gave himself one, pushing the top card from his hand into the center of the table.

Parker's first two cards were a third queen, a deuce —and the ten of spades.

Abercrombie barely looked at his new card. "I didn't make it," he said.

"Sixes and nines," said Duke, "three of the bigger ones."

"Beats two pairs," said Parker. He reached out suddenly, scooped up Abercrombie's discarded hand. It contained ace, king, queen, jack of hearts—and an eight.

Had Parker drawn properly, Abercrombie's card would have been the ten of hearts, giving him an unbeatable royal flush.

"I think I've had enough poker," said Parker.

"I haven't had enough—with *you*," said Fargo thinly.

"Yes, you have," Duke's right hand went under his coat, reappeared with a Navy Colt. "Satisfied, Mr. Fargo?" he asked.

"My fight's with Parker," snapped Fargo, "not with you."

"Mr. Parker and I are partners," Duke said calmly, "like you and Mr. Abercrombie."

Fargo gave Duke a look of tremendous hatred, then transferred it to Parker. "I'll meet you gentlemen again," he said, "when you haven't got a cold hand."

Duke said, "The boat's about to start—and I think you can just make it to the dock—both of you."

Abercrombie pushed back his chair, started at a run for the deck. Fargo stopped to scoop up the coins he had left, then followed Abercrombie. He did not run, however, until he was near the door.

"I guess I've had enough poker for this trip," Duke said.

"You got back your ten thousand," said Parker, "and a little more."

Duke put away the Colt. "That's twice I'm beholden to you, Parker. I'm not a man who forgets his obligations."

"Neither am I," said Parker.

Chapter Five

The trip down the Mississippi was a quiet, restful one. They stayed overnight at New Orleans, then boarded a steamer that went down through the bayou country, into the gulf of Mexico, and plowed its way through heavy seas to the port of Galveston.

Duke and Parker spent two days in Galveston, then Duke led Parker to a livery stable, where a fine team of blacks was already hitched to a buckboard.

"Four days," said Duke cheerfully, "and we'll be home."

They spent three of the nights at roadside taverns, where the stagecoaches made their stops. On the fourth day they got an early start and toward noon Duke said, "Hang on, Parker, we're home!"

Duke flicked the rumps of the horses with his whip and the blacks, responding, went downhill at a gallop. They were headed for a narrow wooden bridge that spanned a stream of some twenty feet. Beyond the stream the road ran between a flourishing growth of cottonwoods.

"Keep your eyes peeled," yelled Duke as the buckboard thundered across the bridge, its rear wheels less than two inches from the edge of the planking.

The buckboard whipped through the cottonwoods, made a sharp left turn, and the headquarters of the Duke Ranch was spread out before them.

Parker had built up a picture of the place in his mind from Duke's references to the ranch during the long trip. He had underestimated the size of the ranch headquarters, even though he had added to it, day by day, reference by reference.

It was virtually a village that he saw now, a village of buildings, barns, corrals, dominated by a two-story white mansion off to the left.

There were at least twenty smaller houses spread out beyond the bunkhouses, of which there were not less than six, all of them of exceptionally large size. The smaller houses were for the families of the married help.

"Pretty, ain't she?" exclaimed Duke.

"Big," said Parker.

"Texas beef," said Duke. "Yankee money."

He laced the horses again with the whip, and they made the final stretch at a dead run. As they approached the big mansion toward which Duke was headed, he stood up in the buckboard and let out a whoop.

People began converging toward the buckboard and when Duke finally pulled it up in a cloud of dust there were thirty or forty persons assembled.

"Hi, Mr. Duke!" calls went up. "Glad to see you're back."

"Glad to see you back, Boss."

"Welcome home, Mr. Duke!"

And the Spanish equivalents.

Duke waved to the assemblage. "Glad to be home, folks. See you all later with some of the Yankee money I brought with me." He jumped down from the buckboard.

"C'mon, Parker."

He started through the crowd, clapping a man on the back here, wringing the hand of another with appropriate greetings, all hearty, good-natured, affectionate.

And then he let out a whoop that made the previous one seem like a whisper by comparison. A girl was flying toward him from the big house. Parker assumed it was a girl since her hair was fairly long, but otherwise she could have passed for a boy at a distance. She was wearing boots, tight Levis, a wool shirt open at the throat. Her hair was of shoulder length.

She was, Parker guessed, when she got close enough, in her early twenties.

"Jim!" she cried as she ran into her father's arms.

Duke embraced her, gave her a quick kiss, then whacked her on the backside. It was a hearty blow.

"Cathy," he boomed, "you promised me you'd be a woman by the time I got back. Here you are, the same old blue jeans. What happened to the dresses?"

"I hate 'em," exclaimed Cathy Duke. "I feel like a ninny going around in that flouncy gingham and cotton stuff. Besides, how can I ride if I've got to worry about the damn dresses all the time?"

"You've got a riding habit," declared Duke. "Seems to me I paid out something like a hundred and fifty dollars for one of those English things."

"*You* wear that—that monstrosity," cried Cathy. "And *you* ride side saddle—not me."

She stopped suddenly, her eyes going to Parker. Duke winced then.

"I'm sorry—Cathy, this is Parker. He saved my life in St. Louis."

Parker started to bow to Cathy, but she stepped forward and thrust out her hand. She had a man's grip, although her hand was very small.

"Howdy, Parker," she said easily. "What'd you save him from—drinking himself to death?"

Duke cleared his throat. "As a matter of fact, it started like that. I was having a couple in a waterfront saloon when some damn crook took a knife to me. I've got a brand new scar to show for it. And it would have been worse if Parker hadn't cut down the knife lad—and his friend too."

Cathy regarded Parker skeptically. "You fight two at a time, eh? You don't look that tough. Bet George Lam could lick you one hand tied behind his back."

"George, eh?" said Duke. "So he's still making sheep's eyes at you."

Cathy let out a snort. "You know what I think of George—aside from his being able to lick any man on the place." She gestured to both Duke and Parker.

"Lunch ought to be ready."

The interior of the house was as magnificent as the exterior. There was a huge living room off to the left; to the right a dining room and other rooms.

The dining room table was big enough to seat twenty-four, but places had been set for only two at one end. A Mexican woman hurriedly put out service for another when she saw Parker with the Dukes.

The main dish for lunch consisted of roast young ham. Duke let out a bellow. "Pig steak! Since when we raisin' pigs?"

"We can't eat beef three times a day," retorted Cathy. "Besides—we can sell beef. We can't sell pork. And I happen to like pork chops and ham for a change."

Duke appealed to Parker. "What this place needs is a woman. Look at her—her face isn't bad, is it? And she's got a woman's figure underneath that pants and shirt."

Parker looked and mentally agreed with Duke, but the ranchman went on heedlessly, "You know how old she is?"

"Shut up, Jim," snapped Cathy.

"Twenty-three!" continued Duke. "Almost twenty-four. Her mother was eighteen when I married her. Keep dressin' like a man, talkin' like one, and you're going to wind up an old maid."

"You go to hell!" snapped Cathy Duke. Her face was red as rare beef and she got up from the table and stalked out of the room.

Duke stared after her. "Now what'd I say to set her off like that?"

Parker shook his head. "I know less about women than she seems to know about men."

"Hey, now, that's a smart observation. You think. . . ?" Duke's eyes became thoughtful and he attacked his food.

Cathy did not return to the table and when they had

finished lunch Duke said, "You'll want a room now, I guess. I'll call the housekeeper and see——"

"No," Parker said quickly. "I'll bunk outside."

"Nonsense, you're staying right here in the house."

"I'd rather not," said Parker. "I came here to work, not to be a house guest and if I'm going to work I'm going to live with the workers, eat with them. . ."

Duke frowned. "Why, I kinda thought you'd work, well, here in the house. I——I had somethin' in mind like a secretary, sort of. General assistant."

"I'd be no good at that kind of work," Parker insisted. "My background isn't——like that."

"That's one thing we haven't talked much about—— you," said Duke. "It's been me——me and my big mouth. You're a helluva good listener, Parker, and you know I'd rather talk than eat. Unless it's playing poker, or drinking whiskey."

"In St. Louis," Parker said, "I offered to tell you about myself."

"I know," Duke said quickly, "and I said to keep it to yourself unless you really wanted to talk about it. You don't——so let's skip it." He hesitated. "All right, move into Bunkhouse Number One. Get the lay of the land, find out how things are done around here, then we'll talk again——about your position here. All right?"

Parker nodded and started away. Duke said quickly, "I haven't forgotten, Parker——and I'm not going to. I wouldn't be here if it hadn't been for. . ."

He stopped as Parker walked off.

Outside, Parker assumed that the bunkhouse on the right was Number One. He strode toward it. A giant about six feet four inches tall with tremendous shoulders was soaping down a saddle outside of the bunkhouse. He watched as Parker approached.

"Is this Bunkhouse Number One?" Parker asked as he came up.

The big man shrugged. "*I* keep my blankets here."

"That makes it number one," said Parker, nodding. "You wouldn't happen to be George Lam?"

"I don't *happen* to be——I am."

"Jim Duke told me to bunk in here."

"Well, go ahead, nobody's stopping you."

Parker went into the bunkroom. It was a large room with single bunks lining three of the walls. There was a table in the center of the room and several chairs. Clothes hung from nails in the wall over the various cots.

Parker found a cot with a mattress folded over and the wall behind it bare of clothes. He straightened out the mattress and when he turned found that George Lam had come into the bunkhouse.

"Where'd the old man pick you up?" Lam asked.

"I met him in St. Louis."

"He win you in a poker game?"

Parker said evenly, "He didn't win me in a poker game."

Lam glowered at Parker. "Maybe he forgot to tell you—he usually does—but I'm supposed to be the ramrod of this here spread. I have to see that the work gets done and I want to know if you're one of the tame cats he puts on the payroll instead of giving handouts to, or whether you're supposed to work."

"I work," said Parker.

"But you'll run crying to Duke first time the work don't please you?"

"Bucko," Parker said, "I'll do anything around here anyone else does."

"What's that Bucko-stuff supposed to mean?"

"A slip of the tongue. A place I worked there was a ramrod called Bucko."

Lam said, "My name is George. You'll call me that —nothing else. Now, if you're ready for that work, follow me."

Lam turned abruptly and walked out of the bunkhouse. Parker followed.

Without once looking back Lam walked past the row of bunkhouses to a corral in which there were a dozen horses. Two or three men were inside the corral, a half dozen outside the pole fence.

A lean, somber-faced man in his middle twenties watched Lam and Parker approach. Lam gave the man a signal and he came toward them.

"Wes," Lam said, "this is one of Jim Duke's mavericks. He says he's real good with horses. Have him gentle a few for you." He looked into the corral. "That little pinto might be a good one for him to start with."

He nodded and, without even looking at Parker, walked away. The man called Wes looked after him, then turned thoughtfully to Parker.

"I'm Wes Conger."

"My name's Parker." He nodded toward the corral. "The pinto's a mean one?"

"Meanest goddam bronc in this year's crop. Threw me yesterday and the day before he stomped Manuel Gonzales and broke four of his ribs. You've been riding many critters lately?"

"I haven't been on a horse since sixty-four."

Conger emitted a low whistle. "George is going to give you the full treatment. Guess he doesn't like the color of your eyes."

Parker shrugged. "I'm not awfully fond of his. Do I saddle him myself?"

Conger hesitated. "Maybe you ought to work around to the pinto. Sorta get back into it with a couple of other horses first."

"I'll still have to ride him, so I might as well try now."

Conger frowned, then stepped up to the corral. "Jose," he called, "put some leather on the pinto."

The Mexican to whom he had spoken showed concern for an instant, then his face broke into a huge smile. He talked to two of his countrymen and the three, mounting their saddled horses, got the pinto into a pocket.

After some difficulty, which they were unable to surmount until the pinto had been blindfolded with a bandanna handkerchief, they managed to saddle the pinto.

Conger said to Parker, "Stay loose and maybe you won't get hurt too much."

Parker walked around to where the Mexicans had the pinto held tight against the corral poles. He climbed to the top, got down into the saddle and caught up the reins. He nodded to the Mexicans who were holding the pinto.

They rushed away, one of them whipping off the blindfold from the pinto.

Chapter Six

Parker felt a shudder go through the animal, then felt its muscles tensing. The horse seemed to leap straight up into the air then, landing solidly on all four feet with a jarring impact.

Once, years ago, Parker had been very good with horses. Once learned, it is an art never entirely forgotten, but he had been away from it too long and muscles were now being called into play that he had not used in many years. However, he was determined to ride the pinto no matter the cost to him.

He held the saddle for almost a full minute before he finally hit the dirt of the corral. He was up instantly, however, and just in time, for the pinto was determined to stomp him into the ground. The Mexican cowboys again cornered the horse and held him until Parker got back into the saddle.

He remained on the horse more than three minutes this time, while the maddened animal leaped, bucked, stamped, and tried to brush him off against the poles of the corral. It finally managed to throw him, and again Parker got back into the saddle.

He was thrown twice more, while the animal's strength held, but after twenty minutes, during which the pinto tried everything instinct and its limited brain was capable of thinking of, Parker finally rode the animal twice around the corral, turning it from right to left, stopping it, starting it again.

He dismounted then and a yell went up from the watching cowhands. He was so stiff and bruised, however, that he could scarcely climb over the poles of the corral. He landed on the outside to find Wes Conger before him.

"Looks like George is going to have to put on his think-cap," he observed. "But don't worry, he'll come up with some good ones. 'Course you might try fighting him. I think he'd be satisfied if he licked you."

"And what if I beat him?"

Conger shook his head. "I ain't seen that happen and I been here two years."

"You fought him?"

"I don't fight—with my fists."

His eyes flicked down toward his right thigh and Parker saw then that Conger wore a revolver in a low-slung holster that was tied down with a leather thong.

Conger said, "He outweighs you fifty pounds."

Parker looked past Conger and saw George Lam bearing down upon them. The foreman came up and without looking at Parker, said to Conger, "The pinto been gentled?"

Conger nodded. "Real good."

"He isn't the only bronc on the ranch," Lam said testily. "You've been two weeks with this bunch and there's another bunch in the west corral waiting." He wheeled suddenly on Parker. "I expect a good day's work from every man on this place."

"Bucko," said Parker, "do we fight here, or do we go off some nice quiet place?"

A gleam came into the big foreman's eyes. "I guess this is as good a place as any."

He whipped off his hat, threw it aside and swung a savage blow at Parker's head.

Parker had just ridden a treacherous bronc and was alert. Lam's punch missed his head by inches. He ducked low, stepped forward and smashed his right fist into Lam's stomach.

The big man let out a whoosh of air, bent forward

and Parker hit him on the jaw with his left. He put every ounce of his hundred and seventy pounds behind it.

He was not in the best of condition after his bout with the pinto, but he had eleven years of training behind him, eleven years during which he had performed the most arduous work that an inhuman mind was capable of wringing from him. He was not long out of the prison camp and the weeks since he had left it he had worked in a lumber yard and his muscles had not yet gone soft.

He was using the muscles that he had built up, that were as hard as human muscles could become. He put into his blows much of the pent-up anger he had built up through the years, the anger and hatred that Bucko Smith had instilled in him.

George Lam was big and he was tough, but he was not as tough as Parker. He went back from Parker's second blow. He remained on his feet, but the blow he launched at Parker as the latter moved in on him was a weak blow. Parker took it on his chest, hit Lam a third blow in the stomach, then, bent low, brought up an uppercut that hoisted Lam into the air and deposited him on his back.

Lam rolled over onto his stomach, started to climb to his feet. On his hands and knees he stared at Parker, his jaw loose, his mouth open. There was utter astonishment in his eyes.

"Up," said Parker.

Lam managed it to his feet. Parker hit him a fifth and final blow. The foreman of the Duke Ranch went down like a steer struck with a sledge hammer. A quiver shook his big body once, then Lam lay still.

Parker looked up—into the eyes of Cathy Duke, who had come up during the fight.

"Well," she said, *"that's* something I never expected to see around here." She nodded. "I wouldn't have missed it for a week of Sundays."

"If I had some whiskey," said Wes Conger, "I'd have me a drink. And I'm not a drinking man."

It was an awkward moment for Parker and he decided that the easiest way out of it was to walk away. He nodded to Cathy, started back toward Bunkhouse Number One. He had gone fifty feet when he heard boots pounding behind him.

Then Cathy's voice snapped, "Wait!"

He slackened his pace and Cathy caught up with him. "I asked Jim about you. He said he didn't know anything about you except that you had saved his life in St. Louis."

"He offered me a job," said Parker. "I asked him if he wanted to know my background. He said no."

"That may be good enough for him," retorted Cathy, "but *I* want to know about you. Who the hell are you anyway?"

Parker shook his head. "If your father asks me I'll tell him."

"You're another one like—Wes Conger. A killer!"

Parker gave her a quick look. He was about to start walking faster when Cathy grabbed his arm. "I'm talking to you, Parker!"

He stopped.

"Jim takes care of his people and the sheriff knows which side his bread's buttered, but McNell's Rangers come through here every now and then. Jim doesn't tell *them* their business. They likely to come asking for somebody named Smith, Jones, Crowdermyer, whose description just happens to fit you?"

"No," said Parker.

"And that's all you're going to tell me?"

"It's all—unless Jim Duke asks me."

"I'll get it out of you," she said.

"Miss Cathy—" began Parker.

She let out a howl. *"Miss* Cathy! Nobody calls me *Miss,* not unless they want me to come after them with a whip. My name's Cathy."

"All right, all right, Cathy," snapped Parker. "I took a month's pay in advance from your father. I'm going to give him a month's work."

Her eyes narrowed as she surveyed his face. "You *are* one of Conger's kind." She nodded. "All right, I learned

that much. I'll get the rest of it in time. Meanwhile—
get back to your damn work!"

She walked away from him, then started running
when she had gone twenty steps. Parker did not look
after her. He continued on to the bunkhouse.

Chapter Seven

During his absence someone had deposited some things on the bunk he had chosen, a pair of grey Confederate blankets, a couple of hand towels, two woolen shirts, a pair of Levis, and a filled cartridge belt with a holster and a revolver.

A middle-aged cowboy sat by the table peeling potatoes. He indicated Parker's bunk with the paring knife. "Rojas brought over your gear from the ranch store."

"That's customary?" asked Parker.

The cowboy nodded. "If Jim Duke figures you're going to stay awhile."

Parker went to the bunk and picking up the cartridge belt hung it on a nail in the wall. He was making up the blankets on the bed when George Lam came in walking heavily. His face was a shade lighter than before and a thin trickle of blood stained his chin.

He said, "I'm not going to fight you again, Parker. Not with my fists."

Parker pointed to the gun in the holster hanging on the wall. "I never carry a gun."

Lam regarded him sullenly. "I fought a man in Dodge City two years ago. He had forty bare knuckle fights in the ring. He didn't hit me as hard as you did." He paused. "I don't like you, Parker, and I don't think I'll ever like you, but I'm going to treat you like everyone else from here on. As long as you do your work."

He started for the door, then turned back. "That fella in Dodge—I licked him."

He went out.

The cowboys began coming into the bunkhouse in the late afternoon. They were mostly young men in their twenties, and even a few younger ones, boys no more than seventeen or eighteen.

The man who had been peeling potatoes earlier was now frying thick steaks in a huge pan and as fast as he had some ready the cowboys came with their tin plates and scattered about the room to eat. There was steak and potatoes, beans for those who preferred them, bread and plenty of coffee. There was no milk for the coffee and no butter for the bread.

Nobody liked to milk cows, although it was said that some of the Mexican women who lived in the individual houses with their husbands and families sometimes milked one.

A poker game started after the cowboys finished their meal. It was for matches, however, for there was little ready cash among the cowboys.

Some of the men had already gone to sleep in their cots when, shortly after eight o'clock, Jim Duke came into the bunkhouse. He had a wheat sack in one hand. It was about one-quarter full, but was very heavy. He hoisted the sack onto the table and it gave out a fine clank of coin.

A cheer went up in the bunkhouse. "Gather round, boys," Duke boomed out. "I picked up some Yankee stuff in Kansas and if you don't want it I'll throw it away."

Duke, chuckling, scooped out double handfuls of silver and gold currency. "Yancey, how much you figure you got coming?" he asked one man.

" 'Bout two months, mebbe a little more."

Duke tossed him five double eagles. "Shorty, how about you?"

"Well," said Shorty, scratching his chin, "I borried some money ahead so I on'y got a month's pay comin'."

Duke tossed him two double eagles, added ten silver dollars. "Call it square."

He went around the group, asking each man how much he thought he should get and added a few dollars in every case. Parker, who remained by his bunk, finally saw George Lam easing toward the table.

"Keep mine, Jim," Lam said. "I'm saving up."

"What for? A big toot in Dodge?"

Lam shook his head. "I'm getting old enough to get married."

"*Getting* old enough?" Scoffed Duke. "Hell, you're *too* old." He suddenly sobered. "Who you got your eyes on?"

Lam got red in the face and moved away from the crowd around the table. Through the gap made by Lam, Duke caught sight of Parker. "Parker, you haven't got your money yet."

"I drew mine in St. Louis," said Parker.

"Hell, that was traveling expenses. It's going to be a couple of months before I get some more money. Better take some now while the taking's good."

"I'll let it ride," said Parker.

"I'll put it on the tally." Duke suddenly came toward Parker. "Hear tell you're real good with horses. That was a mean one you gentled." His eyes flicked to where George Lam was stretching himself out on his bunk. His meaning was obvious. "You come up to the house for dinner tomorrow. Want to talk to you."

Without waiting for a reply from Parker, Duke returned to the table and gathered up the wheat sack. "You all don't go spendin' all that money now, you hear?" He chuckled hugely and went out of the bunkhouse to continue on to the other bunkhouses.

With the ranch owner gone, the poker game was resumed, but it was played for money now instead of match sticks. Some of the cowboys went to their bunks and snores were soon resounding, but those at the poker game in the center of the room were too engrossed in the game to pay any attention.

Parker found that he could not sleep and after awhile got up and went out of the bunkhouse.

40

There were lights on both floors of the big house and off to the right in the married hands' homes there were many lights, although smaller and dimmer than those in the big house. Jim Duke had evidently finished paying the men in the various bunkhouses for there was no whooping or shouting from any of them. Snatches of talk, yes, and from one of those farther away the sound of a guitar.

Parker walked past the second bunkhouse and was nearing the third when he saw a tiny glow of light brighten, then dim; a man smoking a cigarette.

"Parker," said the voice of Wes Conger.

Parker stopped. "Evening, Conger."

"Liked the way you handled yourself this afternoon," said Conger. "That's the first time George ever got licked and it was nice watching."

"You don't like him?"

"I don't like any man who throws his weight around —when he's got the weight."

"What about a man who uses a gun—when he's got the edge?"

Conger drew on his cigarette and it glowed brightly for a moment. Then it dimmed. "I never drew first on a man."

"But you're good?"

Conger countered, "You knew you could lick George when you baited him."

"Yes."

"How are you with a gun?"

"I haven't fired one since the war."

Conger drew on his cigarette again, then dropped it to the ground and stepped on it. "I don't figure you, Parker."

"Don't try."

Conger said, "One thing there's a lot of around here is people. That don't mean, though, that a man can't be alone even in a crowd."

"You're talking about yourself?"

Conger shrugged. "You, maybe."

"I *like* to be alone," said Parker and turning, walked back to the bunkhouse.

Chapter Eight

The cooks in each bunkhouse got up at dawn and their moving about, as they made fires, got coffee to boiling, awakened the other cowboys. With much groaning and complaining they began to get up. Some washed, some did not. All gulped scalding coffee and in a little while ate the breakfast that the cooks prepared.

They were out and about their duties by six o'clock. A herd was being assembled for a drive up the Chisholm Trail. Most of the cowboys went off to work the herd into shape, but the duties on the home ranch had to be taken care of. There had to be a sufficient number of horses in the remuda and the animals, as brought to the ranch headquarters, were in a wild state.

They had to be broken, trained for the work of herding cattle. Since Parker had shown evidence of being good with horses he was assigned to the breaking of the mustangs and broncs. It was bone-breaking work, but Parker did not mind.

The other horse breakers began drifting away from the corrals toward midday until Parker found that he was virtually alone. He started back toward the bunkhouse to get his dinner, but a Mexican woman cut him off. She had come from the big house.

"*Señor* Parker?" she asked.

He nodded.

"Boss say you come have dinner in house."

Parker did not want to go up to the big house, but it was a command and he nodded to the Mexican woman. However, he went first to the bunkhouse and washed himself.

Jim Duke and Cathy were already at the table when Parker finally appeared.

"We were just going to start without you," said Jim Duke.

"I told him you wouldn't come," said Cathy, showing disappointment.

Parker seated himself opposite Cathy. Duke was at his right at the head of the table.

"That herd we're getting together," began Duke, "it's going to be a big one. Six thousand head. I want to follow it up with another in four weeks. I don't want to go back to Kansas this soon and about the only one who can handle the job is George Lam. Or you."

"Not me," said Parker.

"Then you'll have to get together the second herd that I want to start off in four weeks."

Parker frowned. "I've no experience ramrodding a round-up crew."

"You can handle men," said Duke. "That's the important thing."

Parker shook his head. "You must have someone better—someone who knows the work."

"I'll teach you everything you have to know," exclaimed Cathy.

"Yes, you'd love that," snapped Jim Duke. "Riding around all day. But you're not going to."

"I can rope and ride as well as any man on this spread," said Cathy angrily. "Who ran this place while you were away? George Lam?" She made a derisive sound with her mouth.

Duke pawed the air with a huge hand to dismiss Cathy from the conversation. "The Mexicans are the best cowboys on the ranch, but there isn't a one of them's any good at ramrodding."

43

Frank Gruber

"Have you considered Wes Conger?" Parker asked.

Duke scowled. "He's good with a gun, the best in Texas, I guess. Or the worst, if you want to put it that way. 'Sides, he won't take the responsibility. I wanted him to be trail boss on the last herd I sent up. He refused. All right, Parker?"

Parker nodded reluctantly.

Duke chuckled. "Knew I could count on you." He grunted. "Lot of talk, the way you licked George yesterday. I wasn't surprised. I saw you fight in St. Louis. You've got a punch meaner'n the kick of a mule."

"Serves him right," snapped Cathy. "George has licked enough people around here. He had it coming to him. I told him so last night."

Duke shot a quick look at his daughter, then tried to catch Parker's eye, but Parker was looking at his food, fried steak today.

"George decides to stay in Kansas, he's welcome," said Duke. "He wants to get married so bad he ought to get hisself a Yankee wife."

"Well," said Cathy darkly, "I know one Texas girl he *isn't* going to marry."

"He's got more brass than a Yankee cannon," growled Duke. "Had the nerve last night to tell me—*me* —to hold his money on account of he was saving to get married. He didn't say *who* he was figuring on marrying, but if he had I would have hit him over the head with that sack of specie."

"If I'd known that," said Cathy, "I'd really have told him off last night."

The Duke Ranch during the next few days was a scene of vast activity. The cowboys, who would become trail hands, had little to do in getting themselves ready. Their blanket rolls were all they would take with them.

Three chuck wagons would accompany the herd. Three other wagons were loaded with supplies for the almost hundred trail hands who would work the herd northward for eight weeks, crossing rivers, desert stretches, fighting off Indians possibly.

Jim Duke had sent out a call for additional hands. Men came drifting onto the ranch. Some were hired, some were sent on their way with a supply of food and a few dollars. They were saddle tramps, drifters, men on the dodge who would make trouble, but do little work.

Then, finally, came the exodus. The bunkhouses were virtually deserted. Not more than twenty of the bunkhouse men were left on the ranch. A few of the Mexican married hands went with the first herd. Most of them were kept in reserve, however, for getting together the next herd.

During the week Parker caught only fleeting glimpses of George Lam, but the big man sought him out before he rode off to join the trail herd.

"I'm gonna be gone maybe four months," he told Parker. "That's enough time to worm your way into the old man's confidence. I can't help that, but there's somethin' I'm going to warn you about."

"Save your breath," said Parker wearily.

"Hear me out," the big man said grimly. "You been up to the big house and you'll probably be goin' up there all the time while I'm away. Don't try sweetenin' up to Cathy."

Parker groaned and started to walk away from Lam. The big cowboy said savagely, "I told you I wouldn't fight you with fists, but you mess around with Cathy I'll come for you with a gun. And I'll shoot you down like a locoed coyote."

Parker continued walking and Lam half-drew his revolver from its holster. But he let it slide back again.

One of the cooks accompanying the trail herd in charge of a chuck wagon was the middle-aged cowboy from Parker's bunkhouse. In fact, there were only two men left besides Parker in that particular shack and it did not require any order from Parker to get the men to move into one of the other bunkhouses. Parker went with them and in a day or two all the bunkhouses were empty save Bunkhouse Number Three into which the remaining hands had gathered.

The work on the ranch continued. Crews were out rounding up steers. They brought them to within a mile or two of headquarters, where the steers were branded with a big D.

Chapter Nine

The big herd had been gone a week when Jim Duke sought out Parker. He carried a big circular that had come in the mail.

"Read this," he said to Parker, handing him the circular.

Parker read it. It was the announcement of a new shipping point for Texas steers, a town called Lodge Pole. According to the circular it was a brand new town fifty miles west of Dodge City, thus fifty miles less for the Texas herds to travel. There were brand new shipping pens available, every facility for the handling of herds. Plus ample grazing lands to fatten the herds before shipping.

There was a printed signature at the bottom of the circular: General Joseph A. Prescott. Parker's eyes remained on it for a moment after he had already completed reading the text above.

"What do you think?" asked Duke. "Things have gotten too tough in Dodge. The buyers have it their own way. There isn't enough grass to keep a herd fit and you've got to sell for what they're willing to pay. It might mean as much as fifty thousand difference on a herd. A hundred thousand for the two."

Parker nodded. "Aren't Lam's orders to go to Dodge?"

"Hell, a man can catch up to him in a couple of weeks. He can turn to Lodge Pole."

Two men with a pair of spare horses were dispatched early the next morning. They were to carry an order to George Lam, then continue on to Lodge Pole with the herd.

The influx of job seekers to the Duke Ranch had almost ceased. But three days before the herd was to start on the trail a pair of hard cases rode up to the ranch on a gaunt pair of horses. They were lean, shifty-eyed men and Parker would have sent them off, but Duke came up as the men were talking to Parker and he promptly hired them.

"I know," he said to Parker when the men had been sent to the ranch store for outfitting. "They won't be here long enough to do any mischief and I'll ride their tails on the trail. I'm going to be shorthanded as it is. Even by stripping the place of every possible man I'm going to be a dozen men short."

The next day one of the poorly broken broncs which Duke had taken to riding to work them into shape threw Duke. Before the big rancher could get up the bronc stomped on his left leg, making a clean break of the thigh bone.

One of the Mexican women, who was good at that sort of thing, put a splint about the broken thigh, but Cathy was not content with that and sent for a doctor. It took the man more than a day to arrive at the Duke Ranch. When he had completed his work he told both Duke and Cathy the bad news.

"Two months in bed, at least. That's *in bed*. Then another six weeks, maybe a few days less, of moving around easily."

"Three months," howled Jim Duke. "I've got to leave in a couple of days with a trail herd."

The doctor shook his head. "You'd never reach Kansas alive."

"I can ride in a wagon," Duke groaned. "I can take it easy."

"No," said the doctor.

Duke cursed the doctor roundly, but the medical

man remained firm. Outside Duke's bedroom he talked earnestly to Cathy Duke. When he finished with her she was in tears.

Parker was summoned into Duke's bedroom.

The big ranchman was propped up in bed with two huge pillows behind him. "Ain't this a helluva note?" he exclaimed. "Two months in bed!"

"You'll get a good rest," said Parker inanely.

"Rest? Who needs rest? And what about the herd that's ready to hit the trail? Who's going to take it?"

The circular from Lodge Pole, Kansas, was on a table beside the bed. Parker's eyes were on it, for he could already guess what Duke was going to propose.

Duke said, "It's up to you, Parker. There isn't anyone else, there just isn't."

"All right," said Parker heavily.

Duke brightened. "I'll make it up to you. You'll draw a hundred a month in pay and I'll cut you in for twenty per cent of what the herd brings above twenty dollars a head."

"I'm not doing it for money," said Parker. "I'm doing it—because it's got to be done. I'll draw my regular pay."

"We'll fight that out later," declared Duke. "You'll need thirty men at the very least."

"That'll strip the ranch."

"Let me worry about that. There's always drifters coming along. I'll send out the word and we'll pick up enough men to get by. The main thing is to get the herd started. It's getting late in the year and you'll have to push it along faster than you should."

"We'll get started the day after tomorrow."

"Tomorrow," insisted Duke. "The horse remuda isn't quite ready, but they can leave the day after and catch up to you. You'll need every day with the steers."

"Tomorrow," nodded Parker, "so I'd better get going."

He left Duke and went downstairs to where Cathy was waiting for him.

"You're going to take the herd in?" she asked sharply.

He nodded. "Of course."

"I knew you would," she said. "Jim was worried sick about it. Said you wouldn't go to Kansas under any circumstances, but I told him you would." She looked at him, her head cocked to one side, then said suddenly, "What's so awful about Kansas?"

"Kansas is fine for Kansans," said Parker.

"You wanted there?"

"Wanted?"

She made an impatient gesture. "You know what I mean, half the people in Texas are posted in some state or other; GTT—gone to Texas. Your state's Kansas?"

"As far as I know," said Parker heavily, "there's no reward for me in Kansas, or anywhere else and I've got a lot of work to do. We leave tomorrow morning."

He went past her out of the house.

He walked to the corrals where several Mexican horsemen were working over a group of mustangs that were much too wild to be taken with the cattle herd. He singled out one of the men and went up to him. The man was in his late thirties, one of the married hands, with his own house on the ranch. He was the father of several children.

"Your name is Porfirio, is it not?" asked Parker.

"Si, Señor, Porfirio Pablos."

"You know what has happened to Mr. Duke?"

The man nodded. "Is very bad. He is good man, *Señor* Duke."

"He's asked me to take charge of the trail herd. I want you to be the remuda boss."

"Gracias, Señor. I will do my ver' best."

"What's the least number of horses you'll need?"

"Depend how many men you take."

"Thirty."

"Should have five horses each man. Can do, perhaps, with four."

"A hundred and twenty horses. How many are ready for the trip?"

"Ready, *Señor?* Or horses we can take?"

"I know they're not broken, Porfirio, but we've got to do the best we can."

"Have mebbe fifty horses good, twenty-five mebbe thirty not so good."

"Can you scrape together a hundred?"

Porfirio showed concern, then suddenly bobbed his head. "We work like hell on trail. Break horses night. One hundred, *Señor* boss. When we go?"

"We'll get the cattle moving tomorrow. Perhaps we can make eight or ten miles and sort of get the feel of it. You can leave the next day and catch up to us by night."

Porfirio nodded. "Is good, *Señor*."

Parker left the corrals. In front of the nearest bunkhouse he encountered the two hard cases that Duke had hired only the day before. One was a lean, swarthy man of about thirty. The other was several years younger, but looked that much meaner than his older companion.

Parker sized up the younger of the two. "What's your name?"

The man looked at him insolently. "You can call me Brown."

Parker turned to the other man. "You call yourself Smith, or is it Johnson?"

"Depends on who's doin' the askin'," was the retort. "What do *you* call yourself?"

"Parker, and I'm going to be your trail boss."

The man winked at his younger friend. "Well, well, Boss!"

"I asked you your name," said Parker.

"I heard you. I'm thinkin' about it." The man suddenly grinned. "It's Mileaway because that's where I'll be I see a man with hardware on his chest headin' this way. That give you any ideas?"

"I didn't hire you," said Parker. "I wouldn't have if it'd been up to me. But you might as well know right now, once we leave this ranch I'm going to be in sole charge. You do your work, fine. You dog it, I'll run you out of camp even if we're in the middle of the Indian nations."

The men who called themselves Brown and Mileaway exchanged glances. Then the younger one

51

nodded. "Mister Trail Boss," he said, "Mileaway and me was raised on cow milk and we like cows real well. We'll be the best goddam cowhands in your bunch."

Parker walked away from them. There were a hundred things to be done. He checked with the cook to see that enough supplies were in the cook wagon. He talked to the blacksmith to make sure that his forge and equipment were in order, that there was enough iron to shoe a hundred horses at least twice during the trip.

He selected the men who were to work the herd. One or two pleaded to be left behind because of the illness of their wives or a child.

He made a list of the men who finally agreed to make the trip. There were only twenty-four. He worried over the list, talked to a number of the men on it, asked them about those who would be left behind. Were their excuses legitimate?

He could have stretched the list to thirty, but that would have been stripping the ranch too closely. He decided to settle for the twenty-four.

Late in the evening he consulted the list of trail drivers again. The remuda boss, Porfirio, required a minimum of five men to bring up the remuda. That meant that Parker would actually have eighteen men, nineteen, counting himself, to start out with the herd. He ran down the list, checked off the nationalities of the eighteen men. Eleven were Mexican. The remuda men were all Mexican.

The eighteen men included the cook and the blacksmith, who would actually be driving wagons. There were sixteen regular hands.

It wasn't enough, but it would have to do.

Chapter Ten

Parker was in the saddle before dawn. He rode out to where the herds had been assembled. The night riders were still on the job. He roused out the other trail hands, got them to work to moving the smaller herds together.

He had a cup of coffee at the chuck wagon and there found a Mexican named Carlos who had been up the trail four times. He put him in charge of getting the cattle on the road. The man already knew where the huge mossback was who would lead the herd. The animal had been up the trail in spring, had led the herd and been returned to the home ranch to repeat his chore.

There was much whooping and chousing of steers. Riders galloped back and forth driving single animals, clumps of them. The dawn came and the first steers were on the move. A pair of riders kept them headed north, while other riders drove steers to follow the leaders.

The chuck wagon and the blacksmith's wagon were on the move. Riders who would make the trip were assisted by those who were to remain on the ranch. All hands were at work to get the herd into some shape.

It was midmorning before the last clump of steers was on the move. Parker was already worn from the exertions as he fell in behind the tail of the herd. A horse came galloping up from the ranch. It was ridden by Cathy Duke.

"I thought I'd ride with you a piece," she said as she came up.

"I'm not cut out for this sort of work," said Parker, shaking his head.

"George Lam didn't get off himself until the middle of the afternoon," Cathy pointed out. "You're doing fine." She shot him a sideward look, then fixed her eyes upon the rump of the last steer just ahead.

"That's what I wanted to talk to you about—George Lam."

"The last words he had with me were about you," said Parker.

Cathy exclaimed angrily, "What did he say?"

"I can't remember. I wasn't listening very hard."

"Did he—did he tell you that he was going to marry me?"

"That was the general idea."

"It's not true," cried Cathy. "I mean, he—he's been telling people that, but it's not true. I don't even like him."

"Shall I tell him that when I see him?"

She pulled up her horse abruptly. "I don't care what you tell him, you—you. . ."

Parker stopped and turned his horse sidewards so he could look back at her.

"You coward!" she spat at him, then turned her horse and galloped it away. She rode only a hundred feet or so, then made a sharp turn and galloped back to where Parker was again riding behind the herd.

"I'm sorry. I didn't mean that," she cried.

He nodded. "Goodbye, Miss Cathy."

"*Miss* Cathy!" she wailed.

"All right, Cathy."

He touched his spurs to his mustang's flanks and the animal went into a swift gallop. He rode away, leaving her looking after him. He did not look back.

She sat watching Parker and the herd as it moved on inexorably away from her.

The trail herd made eight miles that day, but it was a ragged trail herd, the steers scattered out for two or three miles in all directions. Night riders were put out and they had orders to try to move the animals into a more compact herd during the night but to work easily in order not to frighten the steers and send them pounding back to more familiar grazing areas.

A late start was made the next morning and when the last steer was moving it was after ten o'clock and Parker was taut and angry.

The trouble was with the hands. The Mexicans were experienced. All but one or two of them had made drives up the Chisholm Trail before. The knew what was required of them and the one or two who had not made the drive before followed the lead of their compatriots. The Americans, on the other hand, were completely inexperienced. They were mostly men of the stripe of Mileaway and Brown. They were good horsemen but knew little about working with cattle. And they had formed an "American" clique. They kept away from the Mexican herders and because they were a smaller group they permitted their side of the herd to stray in all directions.

By late afternoon there were two trail herds. The larger one, in the van, was herded by the Mexicans, the smaller one, consisting of not more than a thousand steers, trailed the large herd by a mile or more. And it was a raggedly moved herd.

Parker sent his horse ahead to the main herd. He found Carlos and ordered him to halt the large herd early. He worked with him until the smaller herd came up. Then he called to the American drivers to come together. It took them awhile to assemble, for they were not prompt about heeding orders.

Parker faced them.

"We've made fifteen miles in two days," he said. "That's about what we should make in one day. And we're going to make it tomorrow."

The man Mileaway closed one eye in a long wink. "You run steers you'll run the beef off 'em."

"We're not going to run them," said Parker angrily, "we're going to walk them. And we're going to begin in the morning by breaking up this bunch. We've got *one* herd here, not two and we've got *one* bunch of drivers, not two."

The young rider who called himself Brown held up a hand. "You tellin' us we got to mix with the Mex?"

"There are no Mexicans here, only Americans."

"You loco?" cried Brown. "Hell, half the Mex in this bunch don't even talk English!"

Parker continued firmly, "Every man on this drive is equal. Every man does the same work, keeps the same hours, eats the same food. And any man who refuses to do his job can leave right now."

Mileaway said, "That's big talk you're making, Mister. You got the authority to back it up?"

"I've got the authority," said Parker. "Jim Duke put me in complete charge."

Brown grinned wickedly. "Mileaway wasn't talkin' about *that* kind of authority." He dropped his hand to the butt of the revolver in his holster. "You ain't carryin' no gun."

"I don't need one," snapped Parker.

Brown sent a quick look around the small group of trail drivers. They had apparently not discussed this subject for there were dubious looks on the faces of several of the men. Brown came back to Mileaway.

"What about it, Mileaway."

Mileaway hesitated, scowling. Then suddenly he shrugged.

"Takes a little time to get used to this kind of work," he said in a conciliatory tone.

"You'll get used to it tomorrow," said Parker evenly. "I mean that."

He paused, waiting to see if there was any additional challenge. There was none and Parker moved away from the group. He was aware that the seven men remained together for a few minutes talking animatedly, but soon they scattered and began to drift toward the chuck wagon.

In the evening, after the chow had been disposed of,

56

Parker mounted a horse and started to ride out to visit the night riders. Carlos followed him and Parker, seeing that the man he had put in charge of the actual trail driving wanted to talk to him, pulled up his horse.

Carlos rode up to him. *"Señor* Boss, you are not carrying the revolver. Is that good?"

"I don't own a revolver," replied Parker.

Carlos frowned hesitatingly. "Soon we come Indian country. Perhaps have trouble."

"There are rifles in the wagon," said Parker. "I'll get one if it's necessary."

The wrinkles did not disappear from the face of Carlos. "Perhaps there be trouble—here."

Parker exhaled heavily. "I know what you're getting at, Carlos. Whatever trouble comes up I'll handle without a gun."

Carlos nodded thoughtfully. "There will not be trouble with my people."

Parker went on. He spent an hour riding completely around the large herd, stopping here and there to talk to a herder. When he returned to the camp he found that Porfirio Pablos and his horsemen were having chow. They had arrived a short time before, had built a quick rope corral into which they had turned the horse remuda. There were several head short of sixty, Porfirio told Parker, which with the horses the herders had brought with them brought the total count of stock to slightly over eighty. They would have to watch their horses carefully during the long trip to Lodge Pole, Kansas.

The herd got an early start the next morning. The American riders had apparently decided not to contest with Parker and they mingled with the Mexicans.

The herd made almost twenty miles that day, which put them thirty-five miles from the home ranch headquarters.

Chapter Eleven

Two more good days were racked up, but on the third day the herd began to straggle. Parker, riding into it, discovered that the American riders were again in a group. He dispersed them. By late afternoon they had reassembled.

The herd traveled only twelve miles that day. The countryside was absolutely flat, the grazing excellent. They were nearing, or had already entered, the Panhandle section of Texas.

Parker waited until the hands had eaten their evening meal. Then he approached the group of Americans, of which Mileaway had apparently taken command.

Parker walked up to where Mileaway was seated on the ground, tin coffee cup in hand.

"On your feet," he ordered.

A look of surprise came over the seated man's face. "Well, whaddya know, the big bossman wants to fight." He started to rise, but halfway up threw the contents of the cup into Parker's face.

There wasn't enough coffee in the cup, however, to blind Parker. As the other man came fully to his feet, reaching for his revolver, Parker struck him a savage blow in the face. Mileaway reeled back, still clawing for his gun. Parker leaped forward, struck down the rising gun arm with his left fist, hit Mileaway again with his right.

Mileaway staggered back, fell to the ground. Parker moved in to drag Mileaway to his feet. As his hand was closing on the man's buckskin jacket the roof fell in on Parker. Young Brown had come up from behind him, gun drawn. He had smashed down on Parker's hand with the long barrel of the Frontier Model.

Parker went down only partially conscious. Brown stooped, struck him again. Then he began kicking Parker. Mileaway staggered to his feet, reeled forward.

Brown stepped aside, chuckling, and Mileaway kicked Parker for a good sixty seconds. He kicked him in the face, in the head, in the stomach, in the back. He had to be dragged away by the other Americans.

The Mexicans, led by Carlos, began to crowd forward. Brown promptly shot one of them and the rest stopped. The Americans then went around disarming the other Mexicans.

It was daylight when Parker regained consciousness. Every bone in his body ached, his flesh quivered from the injuries he had suffered, but he discovered that he could not move more than a muscle or two here and there. He had been trussed hand and foot with a hard lariat. He was lying on his back and was aware of much movement around him—yelling, the lowing of steers, the pounding of horses' hoofs.

Footsteps came close and a toe was hooked under his body and turned him over. Parker looked up into the puffed face of Mileaway. Parker's few blows the night before had left their mark on the outlaw, for which Parker felt pleasure.

"Glad you come to, Mister Parker," Mileaway said cheerfully. "Gives me the chance to tell you personally that the crew had a meeting last night—and you know what? We fired you." He chuckled hugely. "Guess who's the new trail boss?"

He kicked Parker in the stomach, which caused Parker to gasp in anguish. "Ain't you goin' to congrat'late me, huh?" He kicked Parker in the face but not too hard.

"That's the way things are done where I come from.

Frank Gruber

You don't like the fellas are runnin' things you hold an election, vote for new fellas. It was unanimous in my case. I got all the votes." He grinned. "Of course we didn't let the Mex's vote. But they're gonna go along with us. Know why? 'Cause we took their guns away from 'em, that's why." He looked off. "We're movin' out so I better get goin'. Oh—I was gonna put a chunk of lead in you but we had a vote on that too, and the fellas wasn't so unanimous, so what the hell, this is what they wanted." He drew back his foot and lightning exploded in Parker's head. He was not aware of how many times more Mileaway kicked him.

Nor was he aware that Porfirio Pablos galloped his horse by a short time after he had lapsed into unconsciousness. Pablos had no gun and was watched, but he risked his life by flipping his knife in the general direction of where Parker lay. The knife landed point first and embedded itself into the ground.

It was the middle of the afternoon before Parker saw the knife. He had regained consciousness a couple of hours before, but was in too much agony to care where he was, or what was around him. His thoughts were back in the prison camp in the piney woods. He had felt this way several times before, after enduring the blacksnake whip of Bucko Smith, the overseer.

It took him a half hour to sever the rope that bound his wrists and ankles. He lay then, flexing his limbs, letting the circulation of his blood take over. Finally, he made it to his knees and then his feet.

He was a mass of bruises. Blood had caked on his face and head. He could not determine if any bones were broken because all of his body was in agony. What he needed more than anything else in the world was a bed and a doctor to attend him. That was out of the question, however, and the problem was one of immediate survival.

He was perhaps a hundred miles from the Duke Ranch. There were no ranches, no towns between him and the ranch. In the other direction it was at least five hundred miles to the trail towns of Kansas. There were no towns until then. There was Indian country, however, and that the Indians were hostile he had been told often enough. A lone traveler would have short shrift with them.

He had no weapon other than the knife that had been thrown into the ground near him by Porfirio Pablos.

Parker had only one asset left to him. His indomitable will that had carried him through fourteen years of captivity in the labor camps of the South. He had also a body that was made of sinew and muscle and bone, a body that had endured hundreds of lashings, that had been built up to sustain itself through abuse and disease.

The body and the brain would see him through this, he told himself as he started to walk—North. The chances of his survival were slight, but Parker could not quit.

Twenty years of the rigorous life had hardened Parker, prepared him for the final great trial.

This was it.

He walked until it was dark. It was not a good walk, actually little more than a staggering reel, but he steadied as he proceeded and the aches in his body became dull throbbings. Shortly after dark he fell down the low bank of a shallow stream and he lay in the water for awhile. He drank some, sloshed his head and face with it.

He moved out of the water, lay down on the bank and slept for a few hours. He woke stiff, cold, his clothes still damp. He got up, washed his face and head, removing some of the dried clotted blood, then crossed the stream and began walking again.

The sun came out and he saw that he was still following the broad trail of the six thousand head of Duke steers.

In the afternoon he came upon the previous night's camp. He found the site of the chuck wagon and the remnants of the leftover food that had been dumped here and there from the tin plates of the trail hands. He scooped it up as he found it and ate it.

He slept and when he awakened, before the dawn, he was so stiff that he could scarcely get to his feet. But a faltering walk soon loosened his muscles.

He had survived twenty-four hours. He would make it, he thought.

Late in the morning he came upon several scattered steers, strays from the big herd ahead, which indicated that the trail drivers were still under the control of Mileaway and his ilk. An hour later he saw the trail herd ahead. It was moving sluggishly and Parker stopped and let it fade away in the distance before he again resumed his walking.

He walked slower now. He did not want any of the riders to see him and every time he caught sight of the herd he slackened his pace.

The sun was setting in the West when he stopped altogether. He waited until darkness had fallen, then moved forward again but in a circling maneuver.

Soon he could hear the lowing of the cattle and the noise of the camp. He circled more and stopped when he was within several hundred yards to the edge of the herd. He dropped to the ground and after awhile made out a night rider. Bent low, Parker advanced. Fifty feet from the trail of the herder he went down again.

Chapter Twelve

The night herder came back. Silhouetted against the sky, with a half moon behind the man, Parker made out one of the Mexican hands. He got to his feet, moved forward.

He was seen by the herder.

"Quien sabe?" the man called.

"Parker," replied Parker.

There was an exclamation and the man rode up to Parker.

"Señor, we t'ink you dead!" the herder said.

"Where's Carlos—or Porfirio?"

"Porfirio with horses, I t'ink." The man turned in the saddle. "Carlos there." He pointed.

"Gracias," said Parker and started walking.

He went a half mile before he saw another herder and approached cautiously.

It was Carlos. He gasped when he recognized Parker and exclaimed in Spanish. Then he bounced down from his horse and grasped Parker's hand fervently.

"You are alive, *Señor* Boss!"

"Just about," said Parker.

"The blessed virgin has answered our prayers!" Carlos crossed himself. "I speak for all of our people, *Señor.* We are not gun fighters, you understand, and our guns were taken from us, but we will do what

63

we can, *Señor* Boss, to help you fight the gringo bad men."

"It's my fight, Carlos," said Parker heavily. "Most of you are family men."

"That is true, but even a man with a wife and children must fight for what is right."

Parker shook his head. "One way or another this herd has got to get to Kansas. I'm going to try to get back control, but if I fail it's up to you and your people to get to Lodge Pole, Kansas."

"Somebody overhear talk," said Carlos. "They don't go to Lodge Pole, they take steer to Dodge City. Sell him there."

"The animals are wearing the Duke brand. No one will buy them without a bill of sale." Parker stopped, frowning. Then he added, half-aloud, "They could forge one. The stake's big enough. They could make a deal with a crooked buyer, a lawyer or justice of the peace." He shook his head and drew a deep breath. "I've got to stop them."

"Porfirio has a gun, *Señor*," said Carlos quietly. "He hide it from them. It only a small gun."

"Get it for me," said Parker. "I will wait here."

Carlos mounted his horse and rode off into the darkness. Parker seated himself on the ground and waited. He formulated no plans. He would have to play it by instinct and reaction.

Carlos was gone twenty minutes. When he returned he stepped down from his horse and pressed a double-barreled .41 derringer into Parker's hand. "Is only a toy, *Señor*," he apologized, "but Porfirio is talking to our people. They will try to help."

"Tell them to stay out of it," snapped Parker. "I don't want them killed in a lost cause." He nodded. "Continue your rounds, Carlos. I mean that."

"But *Señor*. . ."

Parker walked away from him. He circled away from the herd, heading in the general direction of the camp. As he neared it he heard a sudden outburst of wild singing. The ruffians in charge of the camp had apparently discovered the whiskey in the chuck wagon.

Parker went down to the ground. He covered the last fifty yards crawling on his stomach a few feet at a time. He reached the chuck wagon. On the other side of it were the American members of the trail drive crew. They were scattered around, some sprawled on the ground, a couple of them standing.

Barely raising his head from the ground, Parker sought them out. Mileaway was moving around, a bottle in his hand. The young gun fighter, Brown, was also on his feet, his back to the chuck wagon. He was the nearest man to Parker.

Parker came to his feet. He moved to the edge of the wagon, which brought him into the light from the campfire. He moved forward—and Mileaway caught sight of him. For one instant his face was a picture of utter astonishment.

"Be damned!" he gasped.

The whiskey bottle dropped from his hand as he went for his gun. His hand never touched it.

The little derringer in Parker's hand barked spitefully and Mileaway staggered and fell to the ground. Parker gave a mighty leap. He landed behind Brown. His left hand shot out, encircled Brown's throat. His right hand jammed the muzzle of the derringer against the base of Brown's head.

"Move—and you're as dead as Mileaway!" snarled Parker.

The men in the camp become frozen into immobility.

"Throw out your guns," said Parker savagely, "then get up and move back."

None of the men moved.

Parker shoved against Brown's head with the derringer.

"Do what he says!" screamed Brown.

A gun landed on the ground near the fire. The others followed. The men began climbing to their feet.

"Get going," ordered Parker. "You're fired, the lot of you. And you go without horses!"

He shoved Brown away from him, whisking the gun fighter's gun from its holster at the same time.

Brown gave a careless glance at the dead Mileaway. "We'll meet again, Parker," he said coolly.

"Maybe."

"No maybe—we'll meet." The young gun fighter shrugged and started moving away. The other disarmed men began to follow him.

Mexican hands began moving up. The first to arrive was Porfirio Pablos. *"Madre mio,"* he exclaimed. "I see everything. It is miracle!"

"The miracle will be if we get this herd to Kansas," said Parker.

"We make it," promised Porfirio. "We work two times as hard."

That was the way it worked out. The herd was too large for the number of hands and they were up with the dawn every morning and sometimes it was midnight before even those who were not on night duty rolled into their blankets. The men became drawn, lean.

The rivers and streams they crossed were swollen at times, the grass was non-existent, but the drivers kept the cattle moving. There were long stretches without water.

The only thing the herd, and those who rode with it, were spared were Indian attacks.

Some head of cattle were stolen during the long drive through the Indian nations country, but the Indians themselves did not attack the drivers.

Six weeks went by. The grass became better, there was more water. They began to meet riders moving South, trail drivers returning to Texas. From them Parker learned of the proximity of both Dodge City and Lodge Pole. A turn to the east would take Parker and the Duke herd to Dodge. A westward turn would bring them to Lodge Pole.

The returning foreman of a Texas trail drive said to Parker, "One's purgatory, the other's hell. There's no grass at Dodge so you have to sell quick for their price. In Lodge Pole you pay for the grass."

"Pay who?"

"General Joe."

"He charges for grazing?"

"Yep."

"The circular he sent to Texas didn't say anything about that."

"It didn't say anything about his marshals neither. Dodge has got Wyatt Earp, Bat Masterson and Charlie Bassett. But Lodge Pole's got a Pike Massey, Long Jack and Archie Bender."

"They're a rough bunch?"

"You ain't heard of them? Where you from, West of the Pecos?"

"This is my first trip to Kansas."

"That fancy bunch I named is known in Texas. All of them have killed and buffaloed their share of Texans."

After camp had been made that night Parker sought out Porfirio Pablos and Carlos. "Lodge Pole can't be more than twenty miles from here. You can ease the herd along and get there in a day or two. I think I'll ride ahead and find out what's going on."

The two Mexicans exchanged glances. "You go tonight?" asked Porfirio.

Parker nodded. "I've got an uneasy feeling that we may run into a problem I hadn't counted on. If I'm right, George Lam and the boys are probably still here."

He went to the rope corral and, singling out his horse, saddled it. As he mounted Porfirio came up. He had a Frontier Model Colt in his hand. "You take this, *Señor?*"

Parker gestured it away. "That won't solve the kind of problem we may have in Lodge Pole."

He rode off into the gathering darkness, heading north and somewhat to the west. He rode easily, counting on taking his time and reaching the town on the Kansas & Pacific Railroad at dawn or soon thereafter.

He was closer to Lodge Pole than he had reckoned.

By midnight he had come upon a grazing herd, then soon after a couple more. Talking to a night rider from one of the herds he changed his direction to due north and shortly before two o'clock saw the twinkling lights of a fair-sized town.

Ten minutes more and he rode into Lodge Pole.

Chapter Thirteen

Lodge Pole was a brand new town of unpainted one and two-story buildings. It consisted of a single street not more than five hundred feet in length. At two o'clock in the morning it was a busy town. Horses lined the hitch rails on both sides of the street. Wagons, with teams attached to them, were here and there.

The tinny tinkling of pianos came from several saloons and gambling halls. The music was punctuated by whoops and yells of cowhands who were imbibing late and well.

Parker picked out the largest building on the street, a two-story frame structure which bore the name PRESCOTT HOTEL. He found a place at the hitch rail and tied his horse.

He entered the hotel lobby, which was scarcely large enough for a desk and a couple of chairs. A large saloon off the lobby apparently took up most of the first floor.

A dispirited-looking clerk stood leaning against the desk. A half-filled tumbler of whiskey was near his reach.

"I'd like to get a room," said Parker.

"Who wouldn't?" retorted the clerk.

"You're full up?"

The man shrugged. "We got twelve rooms. The General uses two of 'em and we got about fifty people in the others. You can sleep on the floor in one of the rooms. Cost you two bucks."

Parker scowled. "Two dollars for floor space? I'd rather sleep on the ground."

"Get caught and you'll sleep in jail. Cost you twenty-five dollars. We got a vagrancy law here."

"And you've got the lawmen to enforce your laws?"

"The best."

The clerk's eyes went past Parker to the open doorway that went into the saloon. Parker turned. A man at least six feet six inches tall stood there. There was a badge on his vest.

The lawman said, "You heard the man."

Parker said, "I've got a herd of cattle a few miles south of town. The herd belongs to Jim Duke."

The lawman gestured over his shoulder. "You with George Lam?"

"He's still here?"

"He likes our calaboose. We've had him in it two-three times."

Parker gave the man with the badge a sharp look and started past him. The lawman half turned after Parker.

"The name's Long. Jack Long. Remember it."

Parker went into the saloon. A long bar with three bartenders behind it ran down one side of the room. The rest of the place was devoted to tables and gambling layouts.

Although it was well past two o'clock in the morning, the saloon was still patronized by more than forty customers. Because of the late hour the piano had been stilled, but the noise from the imbibers at the bar and the tables, the players at the games, would have drowned out the piano.

Most of the patrons of the saloon were drovers. Many of them were unwashed, unshaven and wore their customary work clothes. Here and there, however, were well-dressed men, storekeepers from Lodge Pole or buyers from the commission houses in the East.

Parker saw room at the bar and headed for it, but

before he reached the open space he stopped abruptly. He had been heading directly toward George Lam.

The foreman of the Duke Ranch had already seen Parker. He had apparently been at the bar for a long time. His face was flushed, his eyes fixed themselves unsteadily upon Parker. There was spittle on his unshaven chin.

"So you made it after all," he said nastily. "I lose ten dollars."

"I've made it," said Parker, "but I've worn eighteen men to a frazzle."

Lam's face twisted angrily. "How much of a herd did you fetch?"

"Six thousand, more or less."

"Six thousand! With eighteen men! How much of the herd did you lose?"

"Thirty or forty head."

Lam regarded Parker angrily. "I started out with six thousand head and lost nine hundred. And two men."

Parker stepped up to the bar and signaled to the nearest bartender. "A beer," he said.

Lam's big hand grabbed Parker's right bicep. "Listen, hero, I'm talking to you. Don't turn your back on me."

Parker looked pointedly at Lam's hand on his arm. Lam saw the look and removed his hand, but his surliness remained. "I've got a score to settle with you."

"We can go outside right now," snapped Parker.

Lam bared his teeth in a snarl. "You'd like that, wouldn't you? When I'm three sheets to the wind? Uh-uh, I got lots of time now that I'm not working for Duke any more."

Parker exclaimed, "What's that?"

"I quit him."

"When?"

"Five days ago. I wrote him a letter about conditions here and he sent back a telegram saying you'd be here soon and to let you decide about things. That's when I sent him a telegram quitting."

"Who's in charge of the herd now?"

Lam sneered, "I don't know and I don't give a damn. I'm hanging around here waiting for my pay, that's all. I told Duke to send it to me."

"Where's Wes Conger?"

"That much I'll tell you," Lam grinned wickedly. "He's in jail, where he'll stay until they hang him."

Parker stared at the ex-ramrod of the Duke Ranch. Then he wheeled abruptly from the bar without even tasting the beer that the bartender had set out for him. He left the saloon and entered the hotel lobby.

"Where's the jail?" he asked the man behind the desk.

The clerk smiled thinly. "Some people can't wait to get in. You're hardly in town and already you want to see the inside of our most prosperous institution."

"I'm not planning to get locked up," snapped Parker. "Someone I know's there."

"Yeah, sure, a friend. Won't do you no good this time a night, but—" the clerk pointed. "The brick building right across the street."

Parker left the hotel and crossed the street to the best-built building in Lodge Pole. It was a low, one-story building built of new brick with a wooden veranda running along the front of it. A sign over the veranda read: LODGE POLE COUNTY COURT-HOUSE, and underneath in smaller letters, City Marshal—Jail.

He pushed open the well-built door and went inside. There was a large room containing three desks, a rifle and shotgun rack, several chairs and, at the rear, a partition separated from the front office by bars and a wrought-iron door. This was the jail.

A wall lamp lit up the front, but the rear section was dark, the light not reaching that far. An unshaven man who might have been a blacksmith at one time sat at one of the desks eating a midnight snack.

He looked up at Parker, but continued eating.

"You've got a man here named Wes Conger," said Parker.

"So?"

"I want to talk to him."

"Come around in the morning. The prisoners don't bother me at night, I don't bother them."

"I want to talk to Conger now."

The jailer pushed back his chair and got to his feet. He was an enormous man with a chest like a hogshead. He picked up a club about three inches thick and thirty inches long.

"On'y way you talk to your friend is inside the kelly —and you stay in till the judge tells you you get out. You want it that way?"

He came around the desk brandishing the club.

Parker had left the street door open behind him. A man appeared in it. He said, "Welcome to Lodge Pole, Mr. Parker!"

Parker turned. The man facing him was in his middle fifties, a lean, weather-beaten man. He wore full mustaches and had the bearing of a military man. He was dressed in gray striped trousers, a ruffled white shirt and a black frock coat.

Parker said, "You're General Prescott?"

The general bowed slightly. "I have been awaiting your arrival, Mr. Parker. Shall we step across the street to my office and have a nightcap?"

Parker indicated the cell. "There's a man in there I want to talk to."

"A friend?"

"He works for Jim Duke."

"He's sleeping now. Talk to him in the morning."

"He's in trouble—serious trouble, I'm told."

The jailer interposed. "He's the man who shot Daly Carter."

General Prescott pursed up his lips, then suddenly beamed at Parker. "We'll work that out in the morning. I'll have a talk with Judge Briscoe. I'm sure everything will work out for your friend. That drink now?"

The general moved into the doorway and looked expectantly at Parker. The latter followed him outside.

As they crossed the street General Prescott said to Parker, "I understand you've brought a second Duke herd to Lodge Pole. We're very pleased that Mr. Duke saw fit to come to Lodge Pole instead of Dodge City as formerly. I'm sure he's going to be glad he made the change."

"I'll lay my cards on the table, General Prescott," said Parker. "Mr. Duke broke his leg just before I left Texas with this herd and I followed the instructions that he gave me, but I've heard some things in the past few days that concern me greatly."

"Rumors, Mr. Parker, circulated by competitors in Dodge. This herd you've just brought—how large is it?"

"Roughly six thousand."

"Excellent!" exclaimed the general. "With the Duke cattle already here, that makes over eleven thousand head, does it not?"

They had entered the hotel by now and the general led the way to a room behind the lobby which was fitted out as an office. The lights were already on and the general went to a cabinet and produced a bottle of whiskey.

"My private stock, Parker," he said, holding up the bottle.

"I'd rather not, General," said Parker.

"A glass of wine, perhaps?"

"Neither, thanks."

"Very well, you don't mind if I have a small one, a sort of nightcap?"

Parker made a gesture and seated himself on the edge of a chair. "You wanted to talk, General."

General Prescott poured some whiskey into a glass and sloshed a mouthful of it in his mouth. He swallowed it, then said, "I understand you have the authority to sell, Mr. Parker?"

"I don't know if I have or not. There's some complication."

"I don't believe so. Mr. Duke's telegram to his foreman, or should I say, ex-foreman, was very clear. It gave you full authority."

"Lam showed you the telegram?"

The general chuckled. "My dear Parker, this is *my* town. There is very little goes on here of which I am not aware."

"That includes the reading of all telegrams?"

"We are quibbling, Mr. Parker. The hour is late and I had hoped that we could conclude this business before retiring."

"I'll probably have to stay up all night," said Parker, "since I can't get a room here at the hotel and the deputy marshal has made it quite clear that I can't sleep in the open."

"Nonsense, Parker, you'll have a room here. The best in the house." The general raised his voice suddenly. "Hogan!"

The door opened immediately and the clerk stuck in his head. "You called, General?"

"Book Mr. Parker in room one."

"Yes, sir!"

The hotel clerk withdrew his head and closed the door. The general smiled at Parker. "Eleven thousand head. Mmm, very interesting. It just happens that there are two hundred cattle cars on a siding right now and the loading pens are vacant. We could start loading tomorrow." He beamed. "Shall we close the deal, Mr. Parker? A flat twelve dollars a head."

"Twelve, General?"

"A good price for this late in the season. And you won't have to haggle with the commission men and hope that they can raise the money to pay you. I'll ship directly to Armour and see that you have the money in full before the end of the week. Eleven thousand times twelve. . ."

"Mr. Duke received twenty-two dollars a head for his last herd in Dodge."

"That was in the spring. It's late now and prices have come down. There's a surplus of beef and the cattle's generally poorer. Twelve dollars now is better than wintering the herd."

Parker shook his head. "I've heard nothing from Mr. Duke since I left his ranch six weeks ago. I believe I should have some word from him before I make any deal."

The good humor faded from the general's face, but he forced it back quickly. "You're a conscientious man,

Mr. Parker, and I appreciate that. Very well, send a telegram to Mr. Duke. We'll resume our talks after you've heard from him. I have your word, meanwhile, that you will not negotiate with others until you hear from Mr. Duke?"

Parker frowned. "I don't think I can give you that promise, General. I work for Jim Duke and I believe it's my duty to use whatever means I can to make the best deal for him."

"Very commendable, sir. I compliment you. In the meantime, if there's anything I can do to make your stay in Lodge Pole more pleasant you have only to command me."

"The Duke hand who is in jail—Wes Conger. . ."

"He'll be freed in the morning. Think no more of it."

The general downed the last of his whiskey. "Hogan will give you the key to room number one. A poor room, but the best we have."

Parker left the office and the clerk was ready with a key. "Top of the stairs, last door on the left."

Parker ascended the stairs to a narrow corridor, dimly lighted by a single wall lamp. He found his room, entered and, striking a match, saw a candle in a holder. He lit the candle.

The room was not more than eight by ten and contained, besides a cot, a washstand and a single chair. Nails in the bare wooden wall served in lieu of a closet. Parker locked the door, blew out the candle and stretched out on the bed fully clothed.

He was asleep in moments.

Chapter Fourteen

Parker's room overlooked the street and the morning activity awakened him at eight o'clock. He washed and left the room.

A new clerk was at the desk in the lobby. He was very young but sported a mustache, possibly to make himself look older.

"Is there a barber shop in town?" asked Parker. "And possibly a place where I can get a bath?"

"Jake's right up the street." The clerk pointed.

Parker found Jake's and for a dollar had a haircut and a shave and was given permission to take a bath in a closet. An hour later he left the shop and looked around for a place to eat. A place near the courthouse and jail had a sign EATS and Parker headed for it.

As he entered he saw General Prescott at the table with a young woman wearing a blue gingham dress. She was apparently in her early twenties. She had taffy-colored hair piled high on her head and was an extremely attractive young woman.

The general greeted him warmly. "Mr. Parker, may I present my daughter Eve? Eve, my dear, this is the foreman of the Duke Ranch in Texas, Mr. Parker."

Parker bowed and murmured a response to the introduction and wished he had not come into the restaurant before looking in. The general was drawing out a chair for him to seat himself at the table.

"Join us, Mr. Parker. We have no facilities for cooking at the hotel so my daughter and I get our meals here. The food is excellent provided you like beefsteak. Although for breakfast you can have sausage and eggs. The coffee is good."

Parker sat down at the table directly across from Eve Prescott. He found her eyes upon him. She smiled. "I understand you've just come from Texas, Mr. Parker."

The general answered for Parker. "Mr. Parker has eleven thousand head of Longhorns, for which I am negotiating. Which reminds me, Parker, have you sent off the telegram to Jim Duke?"

"I intend to do so after I have my breakfast."

"The sooner the better. The vultures will be descending upon you as soon as they hear you're in town. In fact here is one of them now."

A fat little man wearing a derby had just entered the restaurant. His eyes were fixed upon Parker as he came forward.

"I beg your pardon, would you perchance be the foreman of the Duke Ranch in Texas?"

The general exclaimed angrily, "Dobson, have you no decency? We are having our breakfast."

Dobson grinned slyly. "With the manager of Jim Duke's herd!" The fat man reached across the table and stretched out a plump hand at Parker. "Clare Dobson, sir."

Parker ignored the outstretched hand. But he nodded. "How are you?"

"I represent John Speed & Company, the largest packers of beef in Kansas City. I am prepared to offer you fourteen dollars."

"You'll talk no business here," cried General Prescott. "I forbid it!"

"Twenty dollars says you've already made Parker an offer," snapped Dobson.

The general slammed back his chair and got to his feet. "I will remember this, Dobson. Eve, my dear, shall we have breakfast sent to the hotel?"

"I guess we'll have to," said Eve Prescott, showing anger. But she flashed a smile at Parker. "Would you care to join us, Mr. Parker?"

"I'm here, I might as well eat here," said Parker.

The general drew back the chair for his daughter. "Parker, I expect you to live up to your promise."

"What promise, General?"

"Not to negotiate with anyone until you hear from Jim Duke."

Without waiting for a reply the general took his daughter's arm and propelled her toward the door. Not before sending a venomous look at Dobson, the buyer for John Speed & Company.

Dobson dropped into the chair vacated by the general. "A promise don't mean a thing with the general, Mr. Parker. He'll cut you down to size he gets the chance. My company, on the other hand . . ."

"Dobson," said Parker, "if you don't get the hell out of here now I'll cut you and your company off the list of prospective buyers. I mean that."

Dobson opened his mouth to protest, saw the grim look on Parker's face and thought better of it. He got up quietly, moved to the door from where he gave Parker a doleful look before going out.

Twenty minutes later Parker left the restaurant. He stopped in front of it and looked toward the jail just as a man came out of the squat building. The man saw Parker and raised his hand in recognition.

It was Wes Conger, apparently just released from jail. Parker started toward him and Conger came forward.

"Thanks for springing me, Parker," Conger said laconically.

"I came to see you during the night as soon as I heard," Parker said.

"I know. I was awake." Conger was unshaven, unkempt. He was without his revolver and cartridge belt. "You've seen George Lam?"

"Right after I got in. He told me he's quit."

"That makes you the boss?"

"Apparently, although I haven't heard from Duke. I was just about to go to the telegraph office and send him a telegram. Walk with me, Conger."

"Of course."

The telegraph office was in the local Wells Fargo building. The Wells Fargo agent was also the telegraph operator.

Parker got a blank and after a moment's thought, wrote:

General Prescott has made offer of twelve dollars per head for eleven thousand steers. Request immediate reply. Believe price is too low. Sam Parker.

He handed the blank to the operator. The man glanced at it. "Sam Parker, hey—there's a wire here for you. Came four-five days ago."

He skimmed through a clipboard and found a telegram which he handed to Parker.

The telegram read:

Have fired George Lam. Authorize you to take charge of both crews and herds. You have full authority to sell for best price available. Jim Duke.

The telegram was dated five days previously. Parker looked up from it and found the operator studying the form that Parker had just given him. The man was frowning.

"Duke's telegram give you full authority to sell," he observed.

"It seems that way."

"The general's offer ain't a bad one."

Parker regarded the telegraph operator steadily. "You draw your pay from General Prescott?"

" 'Course not. It's only that—" The Wells Fargo man stopped abruptly. "It's your funeral."

"It'll be yours," snapped Parker, "if I find out that you show my telegrams to anyone."

The operator blustered. "Listen, you dumb Johnny Reb . . ."

Wes Conger said, "You heard the man!"

The telegraph operator stared at Conger, his mouth agape. Then he closed it and nodded. Conger and Parker left the Wells Fargo office.

Parker said then, "I think it's time I rode out to the camp. I haven't been there in two days."

"I'll ride out with you," said Conger.

Conger got his horse from the livery stable, where he had left it instead of keeping it tied to a hitch rail. As a result his horse had been fed and watered. Parker's had not, but he got it a feed and a rubdown at the stable and then the two men mounted and rode out of Lodge Pole at an easy canter.

They rode in an eastward direction. From the moment they left the confines of the town itself they saw Texas cattle. There were clumps here and there, carefully guarded by riders. The herds, Parker observed, were generally small, a few hundred head, only now and then one as large as a thousand head.

Parker told Conger of the reports he had heard from returning trail drivers of the general's charge for grazing privileges. Conger grinned sardonically.

"The answer's yes and no. Yes, if you sell to one of the commission men, no if you sell to the general."

"And for us?"

"That was Lam's trouble. He refused to sell to the general, so the general told him that there'd be a grazing charge of ten cents a head. Per day."

Parker looked at Conger, startled. "Ten cents a day for five thousand head?"

"Last time I heard we owed the general about six thousand dollars."

"That's ridiculous. Why, with the steers I brought here the cost would be eleven hundred dollars a day. We'll drive to Dodge City."

"They won't let you—unless you pay what's owed."

"Who are *they?*"

"The general's lawmen. He's slapped a lein on the

herd and it's illegal to move the stock." Conger suddenly raised himself up in the saddle and pointed ahead.

"That's our herd there and if I'm not mistaken that's the marshal's watchdog, there."

Parker had already seen the lone horseman ahead and touched his horse's flanks with his spurs. The animal broke into a gallop and bore down upon the horseman ahead. Conger followed a short distance behind Parker.

The horseman sat his horse, his right leg hooked over the saddle horn. There was a Winchester in a saddle scabbard and a .44 Frontier Model was conspicuous in a tied-down holster. He was a swarthy, mustachioed man.

Parker pulled up his horse. "I'm Sam Parker, in charge of the Duke herd," he told the mustachioed man.

The lawman spat out tobacco juice. "You bring the money to pay for the grazing?"

"We're not going to pay for any grazing."

The horseman bared tobacco-stained teeth in a wolfish grin. "Wanna bet?"

His eyes shifted to Wes Conger. "Thought they'd stretched your neck by now."

Conger shrugged. "They figured the tinhorn I plugged was worth only twenty-five dollars. That's the fine I paid."

"But they didn't give you back your gun?"

"Pike Massey figured it was worth thirty dollars. I only paid twenty new. I'm letting him add it to his collection."

"The difference between a new gun and one you're used to might be worth more'n ten dollars," said the man on the horse. "Your life, mebbe."

Conger shrugged. "One gun's as good as another."

The lawman shook his head. "That reputation of your'n—mebbe it's only good in Texas."

Conger rode forward. Parker followed without looking again at the law officer. When they had gone a short distance Conger said, "That's Archie Bender. Claims he's killed four Texans."

"An officer named Long introduced himself to me last night," said Parker. "He didn't seem partial to Texans either."

"None of them are. They're still fighting the war, which I wasn't even in." Conger sent a quick sideward glance at Parker. "I never asked you, but I figure *you* saw some shootin'."

"Some," replied Parker shortly.

They rode through a densely packed herd of grazing Longhorns and, beyond, came upon the chuck wagons and camp of the Duke herd that had been under the leadership of George Lam. The riders at the camp recognized Parker and crowded forward.

Parker remained on his horse as he addressed the assembled cowboys. "Jim Duke put me in charge of this herd, as well as the one that'll be arriving tonight or tomorrow."

"How many head'd you fetch?" asked one of the cowboys.

"Six thousand."

The cowboy whistled. "We'll have to spread out some then. The grass is getting pretty poor hereabouts."

"We'll move around," said Parker. "I hope it won't be too long, though. I'm waiting for orders from Duke about selling the steers. Then we can all head back to Texas."

"What about some money?" called out a man from the rear. "George Lam wouldn't give us none and he wouldn't let us go into town."

Parker turned to Conger. "Is there any money here?"

"I don't know. George never told me."

The cook by the chuck wagon held up his hand. "There's five hundred dollars in a can buried in the flour. There was a thousand, but George drawed half of it for expense. So he *said*."

"There's that much in the wagon with the herd that's coming," said Parker. He hesitated. "I think it's only fair that you get a day or two off. We'll do it in relays, one-third of you every day. And every man gets ten dollars to spend."

A wild whoop went up at that.

Parker spent an hour at the camp. He sent out a half-dozen riders to seek out the new approaching herd and bring it to the first herd. He consulted with Rojas, who seemed to be the leader of the Mexicans, and arranged with him to release one-third of the hands to enable them to go to Lodge Pole. Parker gave money to Rojas and instructed him to give no man more than ten dollars and to impress him with the fact that he must return to camp before morning.

Wes Conger had obtained a revolver and cartridge belt from the supply wagon, but elected not to return with Parker to Lodge Pole. He had not slept well in jail and intended to get some sleep.

Parker rode back to Lodge Pole. He passed the Wells Fargo office, but did not expect a reply so soon, so continued on to the hotel. As he dismounted at the hitch rail a lean man with a face as hard as if cut from granite moved toward him from the doorway where he had been standing.

"I'm Pike Massey," he said. "You're the new ramrod of the Duke outfit?"

Parker looked at him inquiringly.

"You got the general to spring Wes Conger," the dour marshal went on. "I don't take kindly to that. The man Conger gunned was a friend of mine."

"I was told he was a tinhorn gambler."

"I do a little gambling myself," said Pike Massey. He spat contemptuously. "You Texans have to learn the hard way. Just because you bring a few mangy Texas steers here don't give you no license to go killing good Northern people. That give you an idea how things are?"

"Yes," said Parker, "you want our money but you don't want us."

Massey's face twitched. "As marshal of Lodge Pole I get three hundred dollars a month—and three dollars for every arrest I make. The judge keeps fifty percent of all the fines. I don't mind arresting people and the judge don't mind fining them. In fact he likes it. And so do I. You gonna buck our system? I hope you do 'cause you know what? I think I'm going to like dragging you over to our jailhouse."

"Mr. Marshal," said Parker, "the last thing in this world I want is trouble. I'm here to sell a herd of cattle for my employer and I intend to concentrate on that and nothing else."

"You do that," snapped Massey. He started to turn away, then stopped. "Keep that gunslinger out of my sight."

With that parting shot he started across the street.

Parker continued on and went into the hotel. Eve Prescott was behind the desk, apparently relieving the day clerk.

"How is your room, Mr. Parker?" she asked brightly, then grimaced. "I know—terrible."

"It's more comfortable than I'm used to."

"Tell me about the fabulous Jim Duke," Eve went on. "Is he as rich as people say?"

"I don't know about that," said Parker. "I've only worked for him a few weeks. He does have a large ranch, however, a million acres more or less."

"That's fantastic!" exclaimed Eve. "I've heard that he's a widower, with a grown daughter. What is she like?"

"She's a very pretty young lady."

"Really? I got the impression that she was on the masculine side. Rides and—what do they call it?— breaks horses as well as a man."

"She's an excellent horsewoman," said Parker. "But I certainly wouldn't call her masculine. Tomboy, perhaps, would be a better description."

"I asked Duke's foreman about her—he said she was twenty-four, or twenty-five. Isn't that a little old for a tomboy?"

"I know very little about women, Miss Prescott," said Parker awkwardly.

"Weren't you an officer in the Confederate Army?"

"In the war," said Parker, "my official rank was sergeant."

A frown came over her face. "I've heard so much

85

about Southern gentlemen—the chivalry of the Confederate officers. I assumed you had been a—a major, or captain at least."

"I'm sorry to disappoint you. Would you mind giving me the key to room one?"

She handed it to him, but was still not satisfied. "Father said you acted like a man used to command."

Parker did not reply to that. He went up the stairs and let himself into his room. He stretched out on the bed, intending to sleep for a couple of hours.

Sleep did not come.

Parker closed his eyes and a scene began to form in his mind.

Chapter Fifteen

Dawn was just breaking as the forty un-uniformed, unkempt guerrillas rode into the little village in Eastern Kansas. They had ridden all night and were tired and hungry. There was a little hotel on the single street and the leader of the troop, Bill Quade, intended to commandeer the hotel and see that breakfasts were cooked for his men.

The owner of the hotel, an early riser, looked through the front window at the assembling horsemen, grabbed up a shotgun and running through the hotel, charged out behind it.

"Guerrillas!" he yelled. "Bloody Bill Quade's taking the town. We'll all be murdered!" He fired both barrels of the shotgun into the sky.

Windows and doors began to open in the houses. The inhabitants of the town of Weber, Kansas, had never been visited before by Bill Quade's guerrillas, but they knew his reputation—a reputation augmented and magnified in the retelling. Bloody Bill Quade took no prisoners. He robbed and looted—and murdered. Wherever he went he left death and desolation in his wake. He was the scourge of the border.

There was no point in surrendering to the infamous guerrilla. He executed the male prisoners and his ferocious scum ravaged and tortured the women. Children were bayonetted and tossed about like balls.

That there wasn't a bayonet in Bill Quade's entire command was not known. The Union cavalrymen who had faced Bill Quade's men on a number of occasions had neglected to report that little detail. The number of his men was of chief concern to them. It was always reported as two hundred, three hundred or five hundred. Actually, there were never more than sixty men in Quade's command at any one time.

There were only two-thirds of that number now in Weber, Kansas.

In front of the hotel, Quade heard the shotgun blast, was aware of doors and windows being opened and slammed shut. His men were hungry, however, and he intended that they would eat. He started into the hotel with several men crowding on his heels.

He was in the kitchen opening the food locker when a gun was fired by one of his men in the hall leading to the kitchen. The man came running into the kitchen.

"Yanks, Captain!" he cried. "A whole passel of 'em!"

Quade and his men stormed out of the hotel. The report was true. A company of blue-clad men were coming into the street from the north on the double.

"Mount!" roared Quade.

His men scrambled for their horses. All were in the saddle when the bluecoats, by command, came to a halt and fired a ragged volley at Quade and his men.

Two of three of the guerrillas were wounded, but there were no fatalities. Quade's men began replying to the musket fire, banging away with Navy Colts.

Wheeling his horse away from the hitch rail, Quade rose in his saddle. He was about to give the order to charge the infantrymen when he saw beyond them a troop of cavalry.

Quade decided that breakfast could be skipped, as it had been many times in the past. He turned in the saddle and pointed down the street away from the bluecoats.

"Forward, ho!" he thundered.

It was a wild retreat out of the little village. Quade

led it, but two of his men, by his command, kept to the rear of the galloping column to see if there was any pursuit. There was none for awhile and Quade, leading his command over a rise, saw a wooded section below through which a narrow stream ran.

He gave the signal to slacken speed and when they had reached the woods he ordered his men to water their horses.

They were still engaged in it when the rearguard galloped down the low hill.

"Yank cavalry coming," they reported. "Three-four troops."

The position was a good defensive one and Quade was inclined to fight it out. That they were outnumbered three or four to one did not especially concern him. His men had always been outnumbered. Seldom outfought, however.

The few men who possessed rifles sought good positions. The rest of the command, all of them armed with at least one Colt revolver and some with two or three, saw to their loads.

The cavalry appeared on the ridge above, two hundred men at least. They formed a line of battle, then the officer in command made his grave error. He ordered his men to dismount and fight on foot.

In the hollow below, Quade grasped the tactical error of the commander above. He gave the swift order, "Mount—charge!"

The guerrillas mounted their horses and started up the low incline to where the cavalrymen, turned infantrymen, had taken kneeling positions on the ridge.

The officer above gave his order. A volley was fired from the carbines of the Union men. They were aiming downhill and, like most soldiers shooting downhill, they aimed too high. The volley went completely over the heads of Quade's men. Not one of them was struck.

It was too late to reload them. Quade and his men hit the kneeling cavalrymen. They fought with Navy Colts, their guns roaring and spitting spitefully. More than one hundred Union soldiers were killed in the first minute of battle. The ragged remnants of the cavalrymen got to their horses. They tried to run in all directions. The majority of them headed back for the town of Weber, Kansas. The guerrillas followed, dropping men continually.

At the outskirts of Weber, Quade pulled up his horse and ordered his men to stop the pursuit of the Union soldiers. It took a few moments, for some of the men had followed the fleeing cavalrymen into homes where the soldiers had hoped to find refuge. A house burst into flames as a pair of stragglers came out to join the retreat.

The single blaze, however, did not account for the huge column of smoke that Quade saw from a distance a short time later. Nor did it account for the story he read afterwards in a newspaper—that virtually every house in Weber, Kansas, had been put to the torch. He could only guess that the infuriated Unionists had taken revenge on the village because of their ignominious defeat by Quade's guerrillas.

Their casualities, their commander, Major Joe Prescott admitted, had been a hundred and twenty men. According to the major's report his command, still asleep in their camp at dawn, had been surrounded and decimated by a force of more than four hundred guerrillas who had encircled the camp under cover of darkness. The major had rallied the survivors of the attack and had fought the guerrillas briskly, but outnumbered and outgunned, they had been unable to go to the rescue of the town itself when the guerrillas had plundered and put it to the torch.

Major Prescott's reputation had survived his defeat at Weber, Kansas. He was a friend of Senator Jim Lane and when the senator had been given a division of troops, Major Prescott had been given a regiment with the rank of colonel. He had distinguished himself at Westport in '64 and was given a brigade.

The scorched earth policy of the Union Army made it difficult for the guerrillas to exist as a unit after the Weber, Kansas, affair and the dispersed followers of Bill Quade began to commit atrocities on their own. They were proscribed and hounded by the Union authorities. When a guerrilla was captured he was summarily executed. His friends retaliated with ambushes and murder.

The day of the guerrilla was over and Quade, without followers, traveled to the Deep South and enlisted as a private in a Louisiana regiment.

His unwanted fame grew. By war's end, when he had already been in prison for several months, his ignominy had reached infamous proportions. There were no defenders of Quade. Those of his recent command who survived the war would not admit that they had ever ridden with Quade, much less that they had been at Weber, Kansas.

Chapter Sixteen

        The activity on the street of Lodge Pole increased as the day wore on. Toward late afternoon it had reached a crescendo of sound that finally awakened Sam Parker. He lay on his bed for a moment listening to the noise of the street. A gaggle of cowboys seemed to be galloping their horses back and forth to the accompaniment of whoops and yells.

Parker sat up and then the cowboys added to their whooping the firing of their revolvers. It occurred suddenly to Parker that the cowboys could be Duke men and he left the room and went quickly downstairs.

As he stepped out of the hotel the finale to the cowboys' celebration was being enacted. Three cowboys who had just dismounted from their horses were facing Pike Massey and the tall deputy, Jack Long.

"I told you to reach," Pike Massey was saying. "I'm not going to tell you again."

Parker recognized the men. All were employees of the Duke Ranch, but they were men who had come to Kansas with George Lam and Parker did not know their names. All were young. The one on the left, who seemed to be the leader of the group, could not have been more than twenty.

"We was on'y having a little fun," he protested to Massey.

"Well, you had your music," said Massey, his teeth bared wolfishly. "Now you got to pay the piano player."

His hand whipped down, came up with the long-barreled Colt. He moved toward the little group, his eyes on the youth who had protested to him.

The young trail driver tried to back away but his horse was behind him. He threw up both his hands to stop Massey's advance. The marshal made a sudden leap forward. His right hand went up, down and the barrel of the Colt struck the trail driver on the side of the head. The youth went down like a poleaxed steer.

Massey wheeled, struck the second man with his gun. The trail hand blocked the blow partially with a thrown up arm, but he went down to his knees, blood pouring from his mouth. Massey stabbed the gun at the third man.

"You," he said, "pick him up." He pointed at the first unconscious man. "Start totin'." He kicked the second man in the stomach. "Help him, or by God I'll really let you have it."

The second trail driver struggled to get up. He had difficulty doing so, but he finally made it. He grabbed a limp arm of the unconscious man. His friend helped him and they started dragging the unconscious man across the street.

"Book 'em," said Pike Massey to his deputy. He turned his back on the group, saw Parker, taut-faced, watching. He came toward him.

"Your boys, Mister Parker?" he asked thinly.

Parker nodded. "A little rough, wasn't it?"

"They resisted arrest. They're lucky I didn't kill them. I told you this morning this is my town and you toe the line or else."

"I'll remember," said Parker, "the or else." He turned his back abruptly and walked away.

There was a photography shop beyond the hotel, a dry goods store, then a saloon and gambling hall called the Kansas Saloon. Parker went in.

The place was a honky-tonk with a half-dozen girls,

"working" the patrons. Aside from the girls, there was the usual bar and gambling layout.

Parker stepped to the bar and ordered a glass of beer. Before it arrived one of the hostesses sidled up to him.

"Hi, handsome," she said, giving him the full benefit of a sensuous rolling of the eyes.

Parker nodded acknowledgment.

"Wanna dance, honey?"

"I don't," said Parker.

The girl bristled. "What's the matter with me? I'm not good-lookin' enough for you?"

"You're fine," said Parker. "I meant I don't dance."

"Ain't nothin' to it. I'll teach you. C'mon."

She took hold of his arms. The glass of beer was set before Parker and he picked it up, giving his elbow a flip to dislodge her hand from his arm.

"I'm thirsty," the girl said, changing her attack. "Buy me a drink."

Parker threw a quarter onto the bar, slid the glass of beer before the girl. "Drink this," he said and turning, walked away from her.

"Cheapskate!" the girl shrilled after him.

Parker left the saloon and then saw the lettering on the window that he had not seen before entering: KANSAS SALOON, PIKE MASSEY & ARCH BENDER, PROPS.

The names of the owners were not on the large sign over the saloon.

He crossed the street and went into the restaurant. The roly-poly buyer from Speed & Company was having an early dinner, seated at one of the tables. Parker stopped. He had intended to eat at the counter, but the little man saw him and gave him a glum nod. Parker stepped over to him.

"I can't commit myself until I get word from Jim Duke," he said to the cattle buyer, "but I'm willing to entertain an offer from your company."

"No, thanks," said the cattle buyer.

"You were anxious to make an offer this morning."

"I've had a load of bricks dumped on me once to-day," was the retort. "That's about all I can take in one day."

Parker looked at him sharply. "You're no longer interested in buying cattle?"

"I'm interested," said the buyer, "but not the Duke herd. The general's your man."

"The word's gone around?"

"*You* said that, Mister, not me." The little man's eyes darted to the door.

There was no one at the door, but his meaning was clear enough to Parker.

Parker went to the counter and ordered a steak. It came with potatoes and bread and he ate ravenously and washed his meal down with two cups of strong black coffee. It was dark outside when he left the restaurant.

He crossed to the hotel and found Eve Prescott behind the desk. "All set for a large evening?" she asked smilingly.

"I thought I'd have a talk with your father," said Parker. "Is he around?"

Her eyes went to the door leading to the saloon. "He's in a poker game," she said. "If he's winning I'm sure he won't mind leaving the game and talking to you, but if he's losing—" she shrugged, "he won't be in a fit mood to talk to."

"I'll look in," said Parker.

"Do that—and if he's losing you can take me to dinner."

"I've just come from the restaurant."

Her face showed disappointment. "Then you won't want to eat gain."

Her eyes fell and she reached for the register and began to study the entries. Parker went into the saloon. A poker game was going on near the door. There were five players in the game, General Prescott, the Wells Fargo man, a well-dressed man of about fifty who was probably a cattle buyer, and two men wearing rough clothes.

The general saw Parker and gestured to him. "Mr. Parker, we can use some new blood—and fresh money."

"I'd like to have a word with you—when you're through," said Parker.

"That may be awhile," said Prescott, frowning. "You wouldn't be a real Texan if you didn't play poker."

"I play," said Parker, "but I've got some business to take care of."

General Prescott indicated the Wells Fargo man. "Willard's office is closed for the day. You won't be hearing from Duke until tomorrow."

"Three of my men are in jail."

The man whom Parker had sized up as a cattle buyer uttered a loud chuckle. "In that case, gentlemen, I call and raise you all twenty-five dollars."

Prescott winked at Parker. "On the strength of the fines he's going to collect. Judge Briscoe, Mr. Parker, who represents Jim Duke."

"A fine man, Jim Duke," said the judge. "I met him in Dodge last year. We got drunk together a couple of times."

"I'll give Mr. Duke your regards when I get back to Texas," said Parker. "In the meantime I'm sure he'd appreciate whatever you could do for his employees—the three men Marshal Pike Massey assaulted and threw in jail."

"Assaulted?" exclaimed the judge. "That's a rather serious charge, Mr.—er, Parker."

Prescott said quickly, "Never knew a man yet who didn't claim he was assaulted when arrested."

"I saw it," said Parker. "I was there when it happened."

"Then you had better be in court in the morning," said Prescott with a touch of asperity.

The judge pounced on that. "Ah, yes, nine o'clock. I'll hold court at nine o'clock in the morning and you can be sure that your charge will be thoroughly investigated."

Prescott had given the judge his cue. Parker knew

that there was no point in pressing further at the moment. He nodded stiffly and left the saloon.

In the hotel lobby Eve Prescott was just being relieved by the night clerk coming back on duty. Parker nodded to her, then stopped.

"If that invitation is still good, Miss Prescott," he said stiffly, "I'd like to take you to dinner."

She smiled brightly. "It's a deal—on one condition. That you call me Eve."

"Eve," he said.

"And your name is . . . ?"

"Sam."

"Very well, Sam, I'm hungry, so let's go."

He opened the door for her and they crossed the street to the restaurant. The place was rather crowded but two cattlemen were just leaving one of the tables and the waitress quickly cleared it for them.

Eve ordered a steak medium rare, and Parker contented himself with a cup of coffee. Then Eve said, "Have you always been a cattleman, Sam?"

He shook his head. "I never saw a cattle ranch, not a real producing cattle ranch, until I went to work for Jim Duke. That's a little more than two months ago."

"Somehow I assumed that you'd been in the cattle business all your life. Although George Lam never mentioned your name until, well, until I heard it from my father and asked George about you."

"What did he tell you about me?"

"Nothing, really. To tell the truth, I got the impression that he did not like you. I can understand that, since you were a threat to him—to his job I mean. About all he said was that Mr. Duke had brought you to the ranch one day and—" she stopped, frowning.

They were getting on dangerous ground and Parker decided to take the offensive.

"Your father interests me. Wasn't he, ah, well, a politician some years ago?"

"He was a lawyer, but he hasn't really practiced law in a good many years. Before the war he had a substantial practice."

"That was in the Eastern part of the state, wasn't it?"

"Lawrence, yes. We—we were Abolitionists. Father and mother came to Kansas in '54. From Ohio. I was very young at the time. Father served in the Territorial Legislature, then during the war, well, I'm sure you know his war record."

"Being a Southerner, no," said Parker. He hesitated. "We have our own heroes in the South."

"He went in as a captain and when the war ended he was a division commander, although his official rank was only brigadier."

Parker snapped his fingers. "Wait—I seem to recall something I read once. Wasn't the general the man who drove the guerrillas out of Kansas?"

Eve's eyes flashed as they came up to meet Parker's. "I was thirteen or fourteen years old when that happened. But there've been articles in newspapers and magazines. It's a subject that Father has never wanted to discuss, but he did make a remark once when I showed him an article in, I think it was *Frank Leslie's Illustrated Weekly*. Grossly distorted was the only comment he made."

Parker nodded. "A skirmish becomes a battle, a battle a holocaust when survivors begin to tell their accounts."

"The war's been over a good many years," said Eve Prescott. "It's time the North and the South forgot it and worked together."

"With that I agree," said Parker. "Let's talk about more pleasant things—Lodge Pole, for example. How do you like living here?"

"Father likes it, so *I* like it," said Eve. "My mother died eight years ago and I've kept house for Father —when we had a house to keep. Right now we don't. But in a year or two Lodge Pole will be a settled community. There will be homes, a church even. I'm looking forward to that."

She stopped as she saw that Parker's attention had gone from her to someone beyond her. She turned, saw George Lam bearing down upon them.

He'd had a rough day, no question of it. He was unshaven, red-eyed and very drunk. He came up to the table, ignored Eve and said nastily to Parker, "Didn't waste any time polishing up to Mr. Big's daughter, did you?"

"George!" cried Eve Prescott. "You're drunk!"

Lam turned his attention on Eve. "He's repeatin' hisself," he said. "He's doin' just like he did in Texas. Minute he saw Jim Duke's daughter he started cottonin' up to her. Filled her with a lot of fancy talk."

Parker pushed back his chair and got to his feet. "This isn't the time or place . . ."

"The hell it ain't," snarled Lam. "You've had it comin' for a long time and—" he broke off as he lashed out with his fist at Parker's face.

Parker jerked his head aside, grabbed the wrist of the arm that lashed past him and jerking down on it whirled Lam around. Gripping the arm in a savage hammerlock, he rushed Lam toward the door. The door was open when he started to rush, due to an incoming customer, but the man had swung the door shut and Parker was unable to break the momentum of his rush. Lam went through the glass of the door, taking the entire door with him. He landed outside, his face on the ground.

Parker followed through, his boots grinding glass and wood under him. He stood over the ex-foreman of the Duke Ranch who was groaning as he tried to get to his feet.

Boots pounded the hard earth and Parker, alert, saw Pike Massey rushing toward him. The marshal's revolver was already in his hand.

"Well, well, Mr. Parker," cried the marshal mockingly, "look who I caught red-handed brawlin' in the streets."

"Leave me alone, Massey," snapped Parker tautly.

"I'll leave you alone," said Massey, "in the clink. You coming quietly, or do I have to drag you?"

"I'm not going to jail with you."

"Resistin' arrest?" The marshal moved toward Parker, his gun hand coming up.

Parker saw that there was no avoiding the conflict. He become alert, watched the marshal's arm go up, come down swiftly. He threw up his left hand, took the blow of the revolver on his arm. It was a crushing blow, numbing Parker's entire arm down to his shoulder. But he wheeled and clawed at the gun arm of the marshal with his right hand.

And that was the last he knew for some time. Jack Long, the tall deputy, had been behind him as he came propelling Lam out of the restaurant. Jack Long had drawn his gun and, as Parker caught the marshal's arm, Long brought his gun barrel crashing down upon Parker's head.

Parker was out cold and was dragged, although he did not know it, down the street toward the jail where the huge jailer threw him into the cell.

Chapter Seventeen

Yet when Parker regained consciousness he was not in the Lodge Pole jail. He was lying on his bed in his hotel room. The lamp was on, low, and in a chair, pulled up near the bed, sat Eve Prescott.

Parker's eyes found hers. She smiled wanly. "Hello."

"What time is it?" asked Parker.

"It's after four."

"I've been out—what? Eight hours?"

"Something like that."

Parker turned his head and excruciating pain shot through it. He put up a hand slowly, found a bandage bound tightly about his head, a wet cloth over his forehead.

"It's a very bad bruise, but there's no concussion," said Eve. "I had Doctor Malloy look at you. He said aside from a headache, you'll be all right."

"Who brought me here?"

"I had you brought," said Eve, "from the jail."

"So Pike Massey dragged me there, after all."

"Yes, but it was the deputy who struck you from behind. The one they call Long Jack, although I believe his name is Jack Long." She hesitated. "I saw it."

"Massey struck down two of the Duke men yesterday afternoon. Clouted them over the head with his revolver like—what's his name? Long Jack struck me . . ."

"The term is buffaloed," said Eve. "I've heard it. They do it all the time when a man resists arrest."

"The Duke men—boys, rather, for that's all they were —did not resist arrest. Massey buffaloed them because he likes that sort of thing."

"He's a sadistic bastard," said Eve. "I don't know why Father ever permitted Mayor Ashorn to hire him in the first place."

"Isn't your father mayor of Lodge Pole?"

"No—he doesn't hold any official job. Doesn't want to."

"But he owns the town."

"That's a fallacy. He did own the townsite and laid out the town, but he sold property to business people. He still owns several businesses, but he doesn't own the town, as you put it. But you shouldn't be talking now. You need sleep, rest." She got to her feet. "And so do I."

She started for the door.

He said, "Thanks."

She hesitated a moment, then opened the door and went out.

Sleep did not come after Eve had left the room. Not until the grey dawn began to light up the room. Parker dozed off then.

It was eight o'clock when Parker awakened. He swung his feet to the floor and sat for a moment, fighting the nausea that threatened to overtake him. He won over it, got to his feet. Stepping to the washstand he looked at himself in the small mirror. The bandage had slipped somewhat from its original position. Parker probed about a moment, then whisked the bandage off his head.

He found the bruise on the back of his head; it was the size of a large hen's egg and as painful as an angry boil. He laved the spot with cold water, pressing a compress to it for a few moments, but then dried his hair and found his hat, which had been brought in by whoever had carried him here.

He left the room. His first few steps were wobbly, but

102

then he got his equilibrium and by the time he got down to the lobby he was walking as firmly as ever.

The day clerk eyed him suspiciously as he left his key at the desk, but made no comment.

Parker walked down the street and had a shave at the barber shop. A hot towel on his face refreshed him. It was a few minutes to nine when he came out of the barber shop.

Judge Briscoe had announced that he would hold court at nine o'clock. Parker crossed to the jail and found that the marshal's office was now being used as a courtroom. Pike Massey was at the rear of the room near the cell when Parker entered.

The judge was seated at the marshal's desk. He had a wooden mallet in his hand, which he proceeded to bang on the desk.

"Let's get it over with," he announced. "Bring out the prisoners."

There were twelve or fourteen. Pike Massey unlocked the cell and the prisoners filed out shifty-eyed, bleary-eyed. Several of them wore makeshift bandages about their heads. Several others had open wounds on their faces which they dabbed at with dirty handkerchiefs · or whatever fragment of cloth they had been able to find.

"Court's in session," said Judge Briscoe. "Let's hear the charges."

Pike Massey began stabbing at several of the prisoners. "Drunk and disorderly conduct."

"Guilty or not guilty?" demanded the judge.

Two or three of the prisoners began to make audible complaints. One spoke more loudly. "It's a damn lie. I was mindin' my own business . . ."

"Twenty-five dollars fine," snapped the judge.

"I won't pay it," howled the recalcitrant prisoner.

"Fifty dollars," said the judge. "You want to try for a hundred?"

The prisoner's mouth was wide open. He closed it suddenly.

"I'll pay."

The four prisoners who had been pointed out for the charge paid their fines to the judge, putting the money on the marshal's desk. One of them did not have enough, but borrowed it from one of the others.

Pike Massey, meanwhile, had moved forward five other prisoners. "Disorderly conduct—and resisting arrest."

Three of the five men, judging from the bandages or bruises on their faces, had been "buffaloed."

"Oh-ho," exclaimed the judge. "Resistin' arrest, huh? That'll cost you twenty-five dollars alone—and twenty-five more for disorderly conduct."

The prisoners were very unhappy about the amount of the fine but they were watching a weather-beaten man in Levis, who stepped forward and produced a thick roll of bills.

"It comes out of your pay, boys. You'll learn."

That left five prisoners, the three Pike Massey had arrested in the afternoon and two more, whose faces also looked familiar to Parker. One, in fact, was a Mexican rider who had been with the second herd. He had evidently arrived in Lodge Pole sometime during the evening—and had found himself in trouble within a short time.

"I saved the prize package for last," said Pike Massey wolfishly. "Drunk, disorderly conduct—and resistin' arrest."

The judge said indulgently, "A man's disorderly it follows he's drunk, so that don't mean nothin' special. But resistin' arrest, that's a serious charge." He surveyed the five men before him. "Guilty or not guilty?"

The leader of the group, the youth who had been buffaloed by Pike Massey the afternoon before, looked at Sam Parker.

Parker said, "Not guilty!"

The judge started to bang down with his gavel but recognized Parker. His eyes darted to those of the marshal.

Pike Massey said deliberately, "You a lawyer, Parker?"

"No, but I was a witness to the arrest of three of

these men. You crowded them and even then, when they were ready to submit quietly, you jumped in and struck down two of them. It was deliberate and sadistic."

"Sadistic!" exclaimed Massey. "What the hell kind of two-dollar word is that?"

"I think you know what it means. You tried to do the same thing to me last night, but your deputy had to finish the job for you because you weren't man enough to . . ."

"Guilty!" howled the judge, banging down with his hammer.

Pike Massey waved the judge's action aside. He advanced on Parker. "What was that—I'm not man enough?"

"Take off your gun and I'll prove it to you—and the town."

Massey's eyes narrowed to slits. "You're threatening an officer—in court?"

"We can fight outside," snapped Parker.

The judge banged his gavel again, but it was a weak blow and his protest was weak. "You're out of order."

Neither Massey or Parker paid any attention to the judge. They were facing each other for the showdown.

"No man's ever licked me," Massey said slowly. "I've put down the toughest men ever came to Kansas. In Abilene and Ellsworth, in Wichita and right here in Lodge Pole. I outweigh you twenty pounds."

"Thirty," said Parker.

"I won't fight you in public," said Massey. "I'm a lawman and it don't look right." His eyes slitted again. "There's a new building just finished. Room's completely empty. We go in, lock the door . . ."

"You leave your gun outside," said Parker.

Massey's mouth twisted angrily. He began unbuckling his gun belt. He tossed it to the marshal's desk. "Hold everything until I get back. It won't be long."

"What about these prisoners?" cried the judge.

"They go free if I win the fight," snapped Parker.

"That all right with you, Marshal?" asked the judge.

Massey made a gesture of dismissal. "Come, Mr.

Parker, let's us have our little waltz." He whipped open the door and stormed out.

Parker followed. There was a crowd outside the jail but the townspeople gave way on both sides as Massey and Parker came out of the jail.

Massey did not look to see if Parker was following. He walked a hundred feet to the last building on the street where carpenter's scraps had been piled up in front. The door of the new building was open and as Massey came up a man in workman's clothes came out.

"The key, Mansfield," snapped Massey.

The carpenter blinked. "What?"

"The key to the store, dammit. Mr. Parker and I are going inside to have a private talk and we don't want to be bothered." He saw the crowd that had followed from the jail. "And keep these people away from here. I mean it."

The confused carpenter handed a key to Massey, who strode into the building. Parker followed.

The room he entered was some twenty by thirty feet in size. It was completely empty except for a carpenter's horse. Massey slammed this to one side of the room, then turned and thrust the key into the lock. He turned it in the lock and, removing the key, held it up for Parker to see.

"You lick me, you know where to find this."

He thrust it into a trousers pocket.

Parker sent a quick look around the room. There were windows in front and in the rear of the room but they were shuttered. Enough light came through the chinks, however.

"The fight ends," said Massey, "when one of us is unconscious and that ain't gonna be me."

Parker threw aside his hat and started unbuttoning his woolen shirt. He took his eyes off Massey a moment and when he had peeled off his shirt he looked at Massey again.

The big marshal was adjusting a metal device over his right fist.

"What's that?" exclaimed Parker.

"A little something to protect my hand," chuckled

Massey. "My skin's tender and breaks easy." He held up his fist. It was encased in a heavy set of brass knuckles.

Once during the war Parker had seen a bouncer in a Westport saloon use brass knuckles on a man. He knew what they could do to a man.

"Eve Prescott described you perfectly, Massey," Parker said. "She said you were a sadistic bastard."

"Talkin' finished," said Massey. "It's time for fightin'."

He moved forward. Parker kept his eyes from the mailed fist, watched Massey's eyes. He saw them gleam —and suddenly bent low, his head less than three feet from the floor. He lunged forward.

His head struck Massey in the stomach, drawing a grunt from him. But the brass knuckles sliced along Parker's welted back, searing it as the brass scraped through skin and into flesh. Parker was aware of warm blood on his back and he heaved violently against Massey, using his head and shoulders both.

Massey hit the floor on his back. His hands came up and the mailed fist caught Parker on his bare chest. But Parker was heedless. He had to win the fight quickly, or lose. He kicked savagely at Massey's right arm. His boot landed high on the biceps and the arm was knocked sidewards, the brass knuckles ringing on the bare wooden floor.

Parker pivoted and his left boot caught Massey in the temple. The big marshal slumped. He was not out, but he was groggy.

Parker stepped clear, reached down and with his left hand caught the marshal's trousers belt. With a single heave he brought the other man up to unsteady feet, released him and smashed him a tremendous blow on the jaw with his right fist.

Massey slammed into the wall, slid to a sitting position, then fell over to his left side.

The fight was over.

Parker searched for the key in the unconscious marshal's pocket, found it and, crossing the room, put the key into the lock.

He caught up his shirt, unlocked the door and, flinging it wide, went outside.

The carpenter, hovering nearby, stared at him in utter astonishment. "Here's your key," said Parker. He threw the chunk of metal to the man.

Chapter Eighteen

Parker put on his shirt and started toward the crowd that had gathered in the middle of the street to await the emergence of the winner of the fight. The expressions on most of the faces indicated that they had not expected Parker to be the winner.

Long Jack, the deputy, stood in the open doorway of the jail. Parker went toward him. When he came near to him he said, "I made a deal with Massey. The Duke men are free."

The tall deputy stared at Parker. "You licked Pike Massey?"

"Brass knuckles and all," snapped Parker. "And I'm remembering right now that it was you who buffaloed me last night."

The deputy went abruptly into the jail. Parker hesitated, then wheeled and crossed to the hotel.

The door of General Prescott's office was open and Parker could see, across the hotel desk, that the general was in the office with Willard, the Wells Fargo man.

"Ah, Parker," the general called, "we were just talking about you. Come in."

Parker went behind the desk and entered the office. "You've got a telegram for me?"

"No," the telegraph operator said sourly, "that's what I been tellin' the general. I been on the key since six o'clock this mornin' and I can't get no reply from Jim Duke at all."

"The Duke Ranch is fifty miles from a telegraph wire," said Parker. "He may not get yesterday's telegram until today—or tomorrow."

"He got it yesterday," retorted the Wells Fargo man. "I wired yesterday that it was important and we'd pay the cost of takin' it out to the ranch."

"We'd pay?" demanded Parker.

"I guaranteed it," said General Prescott. "I've a large stake in this, you know. And so have you. Jim Duke must have got the telegram last night. The answer should have been at his telegraph office by this morning."

The Wells Fargo man said, "There's a wire from Duke's local office to Corpus Christi and from there to Galveston. From Galveston it's direct to New Orleans and from there to St. Louis it's no time at all." He paused, screwing up his lips. "Takes three hours sometimes from St. Louis."

"That's it," exclaimed the general. "Those St. Louis people don't get to work at six o'clock in the morning."

"Their office is open all night," said the Wells Fargo man.

"It's still too early to expect a reply," insisted the general. "We're counting that everyone along the line got right on it without wasting any time. That's expecting too much. Give it until noon." He gestured. "I want a word alone with Mr. Parker, Willard."

The Wells Fargo man looked disappointed as he passed Parker and went out.

"Close the door, will you, Parker?" said the general smoothly. "I'm sorry about what happened last night. I've already spoken to Marshal Massey about his methods. I told him in no uncertain terms that he's been a little too, ah, violent."

"Tell him again," said Parker grimly, "after he recovers consciousness."

The general exclaimed, "What's happened to him?"

"We had a fight," said Parker, "in a locked room up

the street. He's still there, unless they've dragged him down to the jail.

General Prescott inhaled deeply. "You—you *beat* Pike Massey?"

"And his brass knuckles!"

General Prescott shook his head in bewilderment. "I don't understand you at all, Parker. You don't carry a gun, but you tackle the best fist fighter in the state of Kansas and beat him. What's your background, Parker?"

"Before the war," said Parker, "I was a school teacher."

"A school teacher? Where?"

But Parker had already said more than he should have. "In Louisiana," he lied.

Prescott's forehead was creased in thought. "You're a man of education then, not like the majority of these Texans. We have something in common."

"Cattle," said Parker.

Prescott nodded. "From what I've heard of Jim Duke, he's a land pirate—well the son of one anyway. His father never bought an acre of land. He grabbed it by force. The Longhorns ran wild during the war. Any man strong enough to round them up owned them. The elder Duke gathered up a band of outlaws and ruffians, gun fighters. He was stronger than anyone else and what he put his brand on he claimed as his own. He made no actual investment in either land or cattle. He didn't *buy* anything."

"I don't know anything about that, General," said Parker, "and I don't think it's any of my business. I work for Jim Duke. He is one of the very few men to whom I owe a debt of gratitude."

"You're still a hired hand," said Prescott ruthlessly. "Does he pay you enough for you to risk your life for him? There's no wage that big, Parker, believe me. Pike Massey's a killer. All right, you beat him with your fists. He'll use his gun on you the next time."

"That's a risk I'll have to take."

"Is it worth it? You can be out of Lodge Pole today—on the train to St. Louis. I'll lay my cards on the table, Parker. I offered you twelve dollars a head for the entire Duke herd. I'll raise the offer to fourteen dollars. That's a tremendous amount of money." A glint came into his eyes. "You won't get any better offer, I can assure you."

"You've intimidated the other buyers."

"I let it be known that they wouldn't be welcome in Lodge Pole if they interfered. Every dollar I ever had is invested in this town. I don't intend to lose it." His voice became brittle. He was talking now as if addressing his company commanders. "I want to remind you of one thing more. Your cattle are eating my grass to the ground. In a week you won't be able to graze a flock of goats within twenty miles of this town. I'm charging you for that grass, Parker, ten cents a head per day. Eleven hundred dollars a day. There's already a lien of six thousand against your beef. At the end of the week. . ."

Parker cut him off. "As soon as I hear from Jim Duke we'll talk about a deal."

"I hope that wire comes today," said Prescott dourly. "I *hope* it comes!"

Parker left Prescott's office and the hotel. Outside, he found a store where he purchased a wool shirt, a new pair of Levis and two or three smaller items. He returned to his hotel room, stripped off his shirt, washed his upper torso and applied some sticking plaster to the scratch caused by the brass knuckles of Pike Massey.

He was putting on the new shirt when there was a knock on the door. Parker opened it to find a glum-looking Wes Conger.

"That fellow Rojas you gave the money to," said Conger, "he's made a little mistake."

"He's slipped with the money?" exclaimed Parker.

"No, no, he's honest enough. That's the trouble. He's been *too* honest. He's parceled out the money you left with him—ten dollars to each man."

"That's what I told him to do."

Conger nodded. "You also told him to give one-third of the men a day off. But he gave *all* of the men another ten dollars."

"And?"

"You're missing the point, Parker. Rojas gave ten dollars to each of the men. So there's now about six men left with the herd. One-third Rojas *let* off and the others, *snuck* off—to spend their ten dollars."

"The Mexicans too?"

"They ain't any different from anybody else. They've had a rough time of it and with ten dollars in their jeans—" Conger shrugged.

"We can't leave the herd unguarded."

"That's why I'm here. But I can't round up forty-fifty drunken cowboys."

"They can't all be drunk."

"Mebbe not, but I just stopped in at a couple of saloons and I didn't see any sober ones."

"Drunk or sober, they're leaving town," said Parker angrily. "Come on, I'll help you."

The two men left Parker's room and going downstairs entered the saloon off the hotel lobby. Although it was scarcely midmorning the place was doing a fairly good business. A half dozen of Duke's men were at the bar and four or five of them were at the faro layouts.

Conger led the way to the bar. He tapped one of the men on the shoulder. "You've had it, Clancy," he told the cowboy. "Get yourself on your horse and head back for camp."

"Hey," protested the cowboy, "my time ain't up. I got till night."

"It's up," said Conger.

The cowboy looked past Conger at Parker, hesitated, then bobbed his head and, swallowing the last of his whiskey, left the bar.

A second cowboy went willingly, but the third put up an argument even when Parker interceded. A fourth cowboy chimed in.

Parker told them, "You'll go back to camp or you're fired."

That won the argument, but at the faro layout Conger and Parker encountered another form of opposition. The faro dealer.

"You cattle pushers can shove your men around all you please when you're with your cows, but that don't go here. I'm running a faro bank and I say who shoves who around."

Conger stepped in front of Parker. "Start shovin'."

The dealer raised his hands from his cards, stared at Conger. The belligerence drained from his face. "Uh, you're, ah, Wes Conger. Sorry, the man who . . ."

"The man who killed a tinhorn like you," snapped Conger.

"I'm, uh, sorry," gulped the faro dealer. "I didn't recognize you right away."

The Duke cowboys, sensing violence, had already retreated from the table. Parker and Conger followed them out of the saloon and the hotel. They stopped to watch the cowboys mount their horses scattered along the hitch rail.

While they were standing there a muffled gunshot sounded up the street. The two men exchanged quick glances and then started along the sidewalk. They had reached the Wells Fargo office when they saw a man hurtling out of the Kansas Saloon. He stumbled on the sidewalk and fell to his knees. The batwing doors of the saloon bulged outward again and Arch Bender, the deputy sheriff, came out carrying his revolver in his hand. He fired at the feet of the man on his knees.

"Up!" he ordered. The man in front of him, blood streaming down his face, scrambled to his feet. Bender gestured. "The jail, Mexican!"

Parker recognized the Mexican then. It was Carlos, whom he had left in charge of the herd only thirty hours before. Conger recognized him also.

"Be damned!" he swore. He swerved abruptly and would have stepped off the wooden sidewalk to intercept the marshal and his prisoner, but Parker threw out a detaining hand.

"Don't, Conger!" he cautioned. "It'll mean another killing."

"These marshals have been asking for it," said Conger angrily.

"It won't solve the problem," said Parker, "and after my session with General Prescott a little while ago, I'm sure I couldn't spring you out of jail again."

"There's only so much a man can take."

"You don't know how much you can take until you've experienced it," said Parker. "I took it for eleven years."

Conger's hot eyes found Parker's, saw the bitterness in them. He hesitated a moment, then nodded. "All right." He turned, continued on toward the Kansas Saloon. Parker followed.

Conger was in the saloon ahead of Parker. He had already come to a full halt when Parker came in. A body lay on the floor, the result of the shot that they had heard from in front of the hotel.

It was the body of Porfirio, the horse wrangler who had been in charge of the remuda on the drive to Kansas. Parker stepped around Conger up to the body of Porfirio. The Mexican lay on his back, his arms outflung. Blood oozed from a hole in his forehead into his eye which was open.

Conger said softly, "Can you take this, Parker?"

Parker exhaled heavily. "I guess I have to, Wes."

"Well, I don't," said Conger. "I haven't liked myself for quite awhile, but right now I guess I hate myself." He turned and started for the door.

Parker called to him, "Conger!"

Conger stopped but did not turn.

Parker said, "Ride out to camp."

Conger turned then. "No," he said. "I'm through with the camp. I'm through with Jim Duke and I'm through with you, Parker. To hell with the lot of you."

He whirled and walked out of the saloon. Parker drew a deep breath and looked around the saloon owned by the marshal and his deputy. He saw a pair of Mexicans he recognized and signaled to them. They came toward him fearfully.

Parker indicated the dead Porfirio. "See that he's buried."

"Sí, Señor," said one of the Mexicans soberly.

Parker left the saloon. On the street he looked for Conger, but the gun fighter had already entered a building somewhere. At least he was nowhere in sight. He had already entered one of the several saloons in Lodge Pole and Parker had no enthusiasm about hunting for him.

He walked back to the hotel, but on reaching it found he could not go into the hotel. There was a short bench in front of it to the left of the entrance. He sat down on it and looked across the street to the marshal's office and jail.

There was the active enemy, but Parker knew that the real enemy was behind him in the hotel. General Joe Prescott.

Prescott could control the men across the street. Or he could unleash them. That he would do the latter Parker did not doubt. The moment of decision would come when he got the telegram from Jim Duke. The general would force the issue then, of that Parker was certain.

There should be a reply from Jim Duke sometime today. Parker would have to make his decision then, to sell to General Prescott for a price far below the market value of the herd, or buck the general in an all-out war.

Parker thought of the consequences of his open confrontation with the general and knew that he could not resolve it with a hope of winning unless he was willing to go to the utmost extremity.

Guns.

As much as he had disliked it he had had to resort to the use of a gun a few weeks ago. Had he not he would not have been here in Lodge Pole today. The trust Jim Duke had placed in him would have been mitigated. He would have lost the Duke herd.

He could still lose it.

At this very moment the decision was being resolved for Parker, although he did not know it at the moment.

Across the street and at least three hundred feet from where Parker sat in front of the Lodge Pole Hotel, Wes Conger was facing Long Jack, the deputy marshal.

Conger had a glass of whiskey in his fist. He had already downed two glassfuls, but they had not had any effect on him. The rawness of his break with Parker was still searing him. More than the whiskey itself it had made him heedless of consequences.

Long Jack said to Conger: "He used brass knuckles on Pike. That's how he beat him."

"That's a lie!" snapped Conger. "If any brass knuckles were used in the fight it was by that goddam boss of yours, not Parker. There isn't a man in this town can lick him with their fists. I saw him beat George Lam to a pulp."

Across the room, George Lam sat behind a table. He was blind drunk. Only the mention of his name penetrated his hazy brain. He raised his head, looked across the room and tried to focus on Conger and the tall deputy marshal.

" 'S a goddam lie," he mumbled. "Nobody ever licked George Lam with his fists."

Long Jack, the deputy, said to Wes Conger, "You can tell that———Johnny Reb friend of yours that I'll fight him with fists any time, anywhere. And that goes for you, but in your case I'll tie one hand behind my back."

Conger threw the contents of the whiskey glass into Long Jack's face. The tall deputy roared in pain and rage. He clawed at his face with both hands, sloshed the whiskey from his face and eyes.

"I'll kill you for that, you bastard!" he raged. His right hand dropped to the butt of his revolver, but then sanity won out over his rage. His hand froze on the gun.

"Go ahead," said Conger suddenly calm. "Draw—I'll give you that much advantage. *Draw!*"

But Long Jack knew Wes Conger's reputation. His hand came away from his gun and the smarting of his eyes lessened from the sudden danger in which he found himself.

"I won't draw," he said tautly. "You got the edge on me, but your life ain't worth a good goddam."

Conger hit him in the face with the back of his hand. It was seen by everyone in the bar. "You're a yellow-bellied coward," said Conger icily.

Long Jack took a stumbling step back. "You're a dead man, Conger," he whispered.

Conger hit him in the face again. "I'm going outside," he said. "I'll wait one minute so you can get the whiskey out of your eyes. Come out then—or I'll come back in here and shoot you down like the yellow s.o.b. that you are!"

He turned and walked sideward out of the saloon.

Long Jack stared after Conger. He knew that he had to go out and face Conger or he would be finished in the town of Lodge Pole. He would never live it down here, or anywhere else in Kansas, for that matter. He was not at all sure that he could beat Conger in a gun fight. In fact he was quite sure that he could not. But he could not back down. Not after taking a glass of whiskey in the face and then two blows with an open hand.

The pain was gone from his eyes, he could see clearly now. He drew a deep breath—and George Lam lurched against him.

"I'll kill him," Lam muttered. "I'll kill the dirty son . . ."

The deputy grabbed the big ex-foreman of the Duke Ranch. "He's right outside," he said. "Go ahead, kill him." He caught Lam's hand, guided it down to the gun in his holster. "I'll back you up. If you don't kill him I'll get him for you."

He was propelling Lam toward the door even as he spoke. Lam had trouble cocking his revolver but managed it as the deputy opened the door.

"I'll kill the s.o.b.," Lam said for the last time as Long Jack shoved him through the door.

Wes Conger was on the street not more than thirty feet from the saloon door when he saw Lam come out, his Colt in his fist.

"George!" Conger cried out. "Get out of—" he was going to add, "the way," but there was no time.

George Lam pulled the trigger. His aim, which was really a pointing rather than an aim, was surprisingly good. His bullet tore through Conger's left side, half-spinning him around.

It was instinct then with Conger. He whipped out his revolver, fired from the hip. The bullet caught Lam squarely in the forehead. Lam pitched forward on his face.

Conger, badly hit, reeled forward to go to Lam. His eyes were on his victim. He did not see the revolver that Long Jack thrust out from the shelter of the door jamb. He did not feel the bullet that tore through him. It was kill or be killed for Jack Long—and his aim was true.

Conger fell dead twenty feet from the body of George Lam.

Up the street Parker had seen Wes Conger emerge from the saloon. He had gotten up from the bench and started toward him, but he was still a hundred and fifty feet away when the final act of the tragedy was played out.

He burst into a swift run then, even though he knew that he was too late. He stood over the dead body of the man of all those from the Duke Ranch with whom he had felt any kinship. A gun fighter and killer Conger had been, but then so had been Bill Quade, alias Sam Parker.

After a long moment he drew in a deep breath and, exhaling, started for the saloon. He passed the dead George Lam but gave him only a cursory glance.

He crossed the wooden sidewalk and entered the saloon. Long Jack was no longer there. The moment he had fired at Conger he had whirled and run through the saloon, leaving it by the rear door.

There were perhaps a dozen men in the saloon, all of whom fixed their eyes on Parker as he came in.

"Who was it?" demanded Parker. "Who was it shot from the door?"

No one in the saloon spoke. Parker had not expected anyone to do so. There was a fear in Lodge Pole, a fear of the law-enforcement body.

"Was it Pike Massey?" asked Parker in a ringing voice. His eyes swept the room. No one would now meet his glance. But one of the bartenders shook his head almost imperceptibly.

"Arch Bender?" asked Parker. "Long Jack?"

The bartender gave no indication that he had heard Parker. He began polishing a glass.

Parker walked out of the saloon.

He stopped again beside Wes Conger. After a moment he bent over and took the Colt revolver from the lifeless hand. He hesitated a moment, then dropped to one knee and unbuckled the cartridge belt. He eased it out from under what remained of Wes Conger.

The time had come for Parker to take up a gun.

Chapter Nineteen

There were four vehicles in the wagon train. The last one was driven by a wicked-looking man who bore the prosaic name of Henry Smith.

In the turpentine camps of Louisiana he had been known as Bucko Smith. He had used the lash once too often, and shortly after the departure of Sam Parker from Camp Three, Bucko Smith had given a man thirty lashes. The man had died.

He already had a black mark against his name and the death of the prisoner was the last straw. Bucko Smith was given his walking papers. He drifted west to Texas, lost the last of his money in a three card monte game and in desperation had signed up with a buffalo-hunting crew as a skinner.

The buffalo hunters began their hunt in the staked plains and worked their way north through the Indian nations. They had filled their wagons a few days ago and were now headed for the closest town, Lodge Pole, where they expected to sell their hides.

Bucko Smith had not liked the work, but he was looking forward now to the payoff, which should amount to close to five hundred dollars for his share. He was smacking his lips, thinking about the first drink of whiskey he would soon enjoy. He gave only a passing glance to the four men who were digging a grave in the little cemetery plot.

He hunched forward on the wagon seat. And then suddenly he began sawing on the lines of his team. He brought the heavily-laden wagon to an abrupt stop, leaped to the ground and ran over to the grave-diggers.

"Parker!" he roared. "I'll be a goddamned Comanche if it ain't the toughest goddam man I ever had in Camp Number Three."

Parker straightened from the digging and regarded the former overseer of the prison camp with distaste.

"So they finally paroled you," he said.

"Paroled, hell. I quit." Bucko Smith cocked his head to one side. "What you doin' here in Kansas?"

"I'm digging a grave," retorted Parker.

"You a gravedigger!"

"Smith!" cried one of the men from the wagon train. "You want your pay get to hell back to that wagon."

Bucko Smith prepared to leave. "I'll look you up in town this evening. We'll have us a drink together and talk about old times. Huh?"

"Talk to me in Lodge Pole," said Parker, "and I'll take a bullwhip to you." He turned his back on Bucko Smith.

Bucko Smith walked back to his wagon shaking his head. He climbed back on the wagon, picked up his lines, then gave the gravediggers a long, last look.

The buffalo-skin train reached Lodge Pole. A sale of the hides was made inside of twenty minutes and the hunters distributed the shares of the skinners. The skinners, as well as the hunters, then began a round of the saloons.

Bucko Smith was roaring drunk by the time he got to the Kansas Saloon. He bought cold tea for one of the percentage girls although he paid for whiskey, and then he went to one of the upstairs rooms with her. The girl came out screaming a few minutes later.

Bucko followed, roaring and threatening to break up the saloon. He was promptly assaulted by the official bouncer of the saloon. The fight wound up with Bucko taking the buckshot-loaded blackjack from the bouncer. He was pounding the man into insensibility with it when Pike Massey was summoned by a bartender and came out of the little private office at the rear of the saloon with a Colt revolver in his hand.

Bucko was a fighter and a brawler, but he had a healthy respect for firearms—especially if said firearms were in the hands of a man who wore a badge. Drunk as he was he submitted tamely enough to arrest.

On the way to jail, however, he kept talking to the arresting officer. "Used to be in your business myself," he told Pike Massey. "One thing I know is handling prisoners. You can ask one of my old graduates." He chuckled reminiscently. "He's right here in town. Saw him plantin' a stiff in Boot Hill as I came into town."

Pike Massey stopped abruptly in the middle of the street. "Wait," he snapped at his prisoner. *"Who* did you see out in Boot Hill?"

"Sam Parker, toughest man in Camp Three. Used to give him ten lashes and he'd take 'em without blinkin' an eye. Give him twenty and he'd put in a good day's work the next day."

"Parker," said Pike Massey, "he was a prisoner— where you were a jailer?"

"That's what I just told you. Louisiana. I used to be overseer in one of the turpentine camps. Parker put in the longest hitch of any man in camp. Hell, he was there from the war."

Pike Massey holstered his Colt. "I'm not going to throw you in the calaboose, Mister, but I'm going to have a little talk with you. About Mr. Parker."

An hour later Massey sat in his private office at the rear of the Kansas Saloon. With him were his deputies, Arch Bender and Long Jack. He told them of what he had learned from Bucko Smith, the former prison camp overseer. He saved the choicest morsel for last.

"His name isn't Parker. Smith says he got it from one of the prisoners once, a man who was trying to get out of thirty lashes. Want to make a guess who our friend Parker really is?"

"Jefferson Davis?" said Bender sarcastically.

"You're close. Our man used to be almost as well known. Especially in Kansas—up in the northeast part. And they hate him there more'n they ever hated Jeff Davis." Pike Massey smacked his lips. "They remember Bill Quade up there—and they got a special rope they been saving to hang him with."

The two deputies stared at Pike Massey. Long Jack finally said, "Bloody Bill was killed at Westport during the war."

"Was he?" asked Pike Massey. "He was also killed in Kentucky and then again, depending on which story you've heard or read, he went back to Ohio and is teachin' school."

"There's a man here in town who ought to know Bloody Bill," said Arch Bender thoughtfully. "General Joe Prescott. Bloody Bill shot the hell out of Prescott and his cavalry."

"They didn't meet face to face," said Pike Massey, "and from what I've heard of that Weber affair, the bluecoats was too busy running to get a good look at Quade and his boys."

"I know a man who rode with Bloody Bill," said Long Jack. "I never asked him to his face if he had, but where there's smoke you usually find somethin' burnin'." He paused. "Santa Fe Shaw was with Bill Quade."

Pike Massey's eyes narrowed. "Seems to me I've heard that same rumor." He nodded thoughtfully. "Mebbe that's where he learned his trade."

Arch Bender grunted. "Why don't we arrange a little meetin' between Santa Fe and his old captain?"

"All we have to do is find Santa Fe," said Long Jack.

"That shouldn't be hard," Pike Massey said. "He was in Dodge ten days ago when I was there."

"They've probably run him out of town by now," said Bender.

Massey shook his head. "Who'd run Santa Fe Shaw out of town if he didn't want to go?"

"Not me," said Long Jack promptly, "not unless I wanted to be number twenty-three, or is it thirty-three? If Santa Fe put notches in his gun for every man he's planted there wouldn't be any wood left on the handle."

Massey entered the Wells Fargo office and closed the street door behind him.

"I want to send a telegram, Willard," he told the Wells Fargo man.

"Sure thing, Marshal."

Massey picked up a pencil, moistened the lead with his tongue and wrote out his telegram:

Santa Fe Shaw
Dodge City, Kansas

Can pay you two thousand dollars if you come at once to Lodge Pole.

Pike Massey, Marshal

The telegraph operator began reading the telegram. He read the name on it silently, then repeated it aloud. "Santa Fe Shaw, why, that's the . . ."

"Willard," said Pike Massey, "when you send this telegram I want you to tear up this hunk of paper. And if the general hears about it I'll know who told him. Understand?"

"I understand," said Willard, "but . . ."

"You heard me," said Massey and turning, walked out of the Wells Fargo office.

Willard stared after Massey, then turning, stepped to the key. Before he touched it the instrument began clicking. He acknowledged that he was ready to receive, then listened as the message came through.

It was dark in Parker's room, but he had not bothered to light the lamp. He had not eaten supper, but he was not hungry.

There was a knock on the door. Parker rolled his head sideward, but made no move to get up. The knock was repeated.

"It's me, Eve Prescott! I know you're inside."

Wearily he swung his feet to the floor. He found a match, struck it and lit the lamp.

Eve spoke again from the other side of the door. "Please, Sam, I want to talk to you."

He shot back the bolt on the door and opened it. Eve came in, closed the door and leaned with her back against it.

"I heard what happened," she said, "and I've a good idea of how you feel. But it doesn't do any good to sit here in your room and brood."

"Brood?"

"Isn't that what you've been doing? They were employees of yours and you feel responsible."

"One thing I wasn't doing," said Parker, "is brooding."

"Then take me to supper. I know you haven't had yours because I was waiting downstairs."

"I don't think I'd be fit company," said Parker, then added quickly, "and not because I'm brooding."

"You've got problems," said Eve. "Who hasn't? Let's talk about both of our problems over supper. And if I have to give you an inducement, all right. I'll tell you something that I think you would like to know. Something that'll put you in a better mood."

Parker saw that she was determined and he picked up his hat and they left the room. On the way downstairs Eve said to him, "I've had a long session with Father. He's a stubborn man, but I know how to work him around to things. He's agreed to let me go to St. Louis for the winter."

"Is that what you want to do?"

Eve shuddered. "Would you want to spend a winter here? There won't be any more cattle drives coming here after a couple or three more weeks, and this town will roll over and die. Until spring anyway. But that isn't the good news I was going to give you."

She did not tell him more, however, until they had entered the restaurant and ordered their meals. Then she planted her elbows on the table and clasping her hands together, smiled across them at Parker.

"He's agreed to raise his price for your steers," she

126

said. "Sixteen dollars per head." Then she added quickly. "And no grazing charges!"

He looked at her thoughtfully. "He's asked you to talk to me?"

The forced cheerfulness faded from her face. "I don't think I like that."

"I'm sorry," Parker said. "I warned you I wasn't good company."

"I thought you'd be glad to hear it from me," she said. "You and Father haven't—well, let's face it— you haven't got along well at all."

A brittleness came into her voice. "I'm supposed to keep my eyes closed and my ears shut about the things that happen in this town. I'm a woman first of all and, second, I'm General Prescott's daughter. I mustn't know about the—the *sordid* things in Lodge Pole. But because I *am* General Prescott's daughter I *must* know the things that are happening in—in this town. I know that you had a fight with Pike Massey this morning and I—I saw the gun that you're carrying now. You blame Massey for what happened to your friends today and you're going to shoot it out with him." She stopped, then said fiercely, "Aren't you?"

Parker said, "I don't think that's a subject we can discuss."

"What can we talk about then?" She looked at him steadily, her eyes unyielding. "You—and me?"

He stared at her.

"All right, let's talk about it. You're a man—I'm a woman."

"Good Lord," whispered Parker.

There was a tinge of red in both of her cheeks. "We've known each other two days," she went on. "It isn't very long but a—a woman can tell." She stopped until she saw that his face was tightening even more than it usually did. "You do—like me?"

He said, "You don't know a thing about me."

"I know more than you think I do. You told Father that you were a schoolteacher before the war. All right, you've had a hard life since the war. A good many Southerners have, but they still have to live their lives and you can't live on bitterness and hatred alone. That —that's why I told you I was going to St. Louis for the winter. I—I thought perhaps you could go there too. You could find something there to do, something more civilized than what you've been doing and I—I thought, well, that we would have a chance to get really acquainted before we—" Her words trailed off as she saw that the bleakness in his face was becoming heavier.

The arrival of their food gave Parker a brief respite, but when the waiter had gone he found her eyes still on him waiting—waiting for some response from him.

He said slowly, "A man came to town this afternoon. He's probably looking for me right now to—to reminisce about old times. The man's name is Smith, but we knew him as Bucko Smith when he was the overseer in a prison work camp in Louisiana—" he paused, "where I was a prisoner . . ."

Eve cried out poignantly, "You—a convict?"

"An incorrigible. Do you want to know how *long* I was in prison?"

Her eyes fell from his finally and she picked up a knife and put a piece of beef stew into her mouth. She chewed it with her eyes on her plate. Then she swallowed and looked up at him.

"You're trying to shock me," she said.

"I told you yesterday that I didn't know anything about women," he said. "Because that was one thing they didn't teach us in the piney woods."

He stopped. Eve had pushed back her chair. She got up and left the restaurant. Parker waited two minutes, then paid for his meal and Eve's and left the restaurant.

Chapter Twenty

There was a back door to General Prescott's office which opened on the alley behind the hotel. The general was at his desk adding his assets as nearly as he could determine them, when there was a furtive tap on the back door.

"Who is it?" exclaimed the general.

"Willard," came a low reply.

Annoyed, the general got up and shot back the bolt on the door. "Why can't you come around the front like everybody else?" he demanded.

"I didn't want anyone to know I was coming here," replied Willard. "I got a private message for you. That telegram Parker sent to Jim Duke—there won't be any reply to it."

"Why not?"

" 'Cause Jim Duke isn't home. I had a tracer put on it. Jim Duke left the ranch six days ago. They said at his house that he was coming to Kansas."

"Here?" exclaimed the general. Then, "Of course, where else?"

"They said he was comin' upriver."

"To St. Louis. Then by train," the general nodded thoughtfully. "He might be here at any time then." He paused. "Does Parker know Duke's coming?"

"I haven't told him. Thought maybe you might want to keep that to yourself."

129

"Perhaps I do. I'll give it some thought. Thanks, Willard. I appreciate your telling me."

It was a dismissal, but Willard was not ready to go.

The general looked at him sharply. "Something else?"

"Yes, sir, but I don't exactly know how to put it."

"Just spill it. I'll sort it out."

"It's not that easy, sir. I—I've been threatened."

"By who?" snapped General Prescott.

The unhappy Willard now wished he had not started on this subject. "It's a—telegram Marshal Massey sent off. He—he told me particularly that I wasn't to tell you about it."

That was the wrong thing to say to the general. "Massey takes on a little too much for himself. He isn't indispensable by any means. Especially after what's happened here today. Out with it, Willard!"

"He's sent for Santa Fe Shaw."

"Santa Fe. Isn't that the notorious outlaw?"

"I don't think he's considered an outlaw, General," said Willard. "A gun fighter, yes—the best in the country."

"Or worst," snapped the general. "There's no such thing as a *good* gun fighter. Damn it, haven't we got enough of that kind here now? Do we have to *import* gun fighters?"

"I think Marshal Massey's bringing Shaw here to kill Parker," offered Willard. "He—he offered him two thousand dollars to come at once."

The general stared at the Wells Fargo man.

Parker walked the short street of Lodge Pole. He went down one side of the street, then back on the other side. There was plenty of light from the saloons and the stores so that he could identify the faces of the people he passed. The law-enforcement body of Lodge Pole was not roaming the street this evening.

It was an hour after his abortive supper with Eve Prescott when he finally turned in to the hotel to find General Prescott seated in his office, the door open.

"Parker," the general called, "I've been waiting for you to show up."

Parker was in no mood for another session with the general. He shot a glance at the stairs, then shrugged and went behind the desk into Prescott's office.

There was a bottle of whiskey on the desk, a half-filled glass beside it. A big cigar was champed in Prescott's mouth.

"You had dinner with my daughter," Prescott began. "I saw her for a minute when she got back. She said she told you about my new offer for the Duke beef. My last and final offer."

"I still haven't received an answer from Jim Duke," said Parker.

"I haven't heard from him either," said Prescott. "Willard's telegraphed two or three times trying to get an answer. He hasn't got one. But you don't need him to close the deal with me. The offer I made you's a good one. You couldn't get a better from anyone else. It's important that we close the deal tonight."

"I said I would wait for Jim Duke's answer."

"Dammit, man, you *can't* wait. I've been sitting here for an hour figuring how I could put it to you." Prescott scooped up the whiskey glass and tossed the contents down his throat. He wiped his mouth with the back of his hand and set the glass back on the desk.

"The sooner you leave town the better. And by soon I mean tonight. Is that plain enough?"

"No," said Parker quietly.

"Then I'll give you the other barrel. You've made some enemies in this town, Parker. One of those enemies is offering a two thousand dollar bounty on your head. Is that clear enough?"

"Pike Massey?" asked Parker.

"I've told you more'n I should already. I got that piece of information from Willard, the telegraph operator. You've got time to get away. Just sign this paper closing the deal and the money'll be ready for you in St. Louis by the time you get there."

"General," said Parker evenly, "I've had a hard day of it. I think I'll turn in."

"You can't," cried Prescott, pushing back his chair and springing to his feet.

"Yes, I can," said Parker and left the office.

Chapter Twenty-one

Pike Massey spent the night in his office in the jailhouse. About six o'clock he was dozing in his chair behind the marshal's desk when the street door opened and a man came in. Massey became wide-awake.

The man who had entered was a lean, weather-beaten man of about thirty-one or two. He wore a short heavy coat that did not conceal the gun and holster on his right thigh. The holster was tied down with a rawhide thong.

He gave Pike Massey a half-salute. "You sent for me, Pike?"

Massey indicated a chair. "I offered you two thousand dollars to come here. Naturally I expect something in return."

Santa Fe Shaw shrugged carelessly. "Of course."

He looked at the chair offered to him and sat down.

"I want to ask you something personal," Massey went on. "There's no need to get mad about it 'cause it's, well, kind of important to me."

"Ask," said Santa Fe Shaw. "I don't have to answer."

"I've heard talk now and then that you rode with Bloody Bill during the war."

Santa Fe Shaw smiled pleasantly. "Give a dog a bad name . . ."

"I'll change the question," said Massey. "Would you know Bill Quade if you saw him?"

"How could I know him? He's dead."

"Would you know him if he were alive?"

Santa Fe Shaw studied Massey's face thoughtfully. "I guess you got something up your sleeve, all right. That two thousand dollars—do I get it for identifying a picture of Bill Quade?"

"You get it for killing him," said Massey coldly.

Santa Fe took a thin cigar from inside his coat, struck a match and lit the cigar. "Pike," he said, "you sent me a telegram and I rode all night to get here because you made it sound *urgent.* I don't take kindly to bein' made a fool of. I think you know my reputation well enough for that."

"I know your reputation," said Massey. "You're a gun fighter. You've killed a lot of people."

"As to that," said Santa Fe Shaw, "what about yourself?"

Pike Massey made an impatient gesture. "We're talkin' cold turkey. I asked you two questions and you haven't given me an answer to even one of them."

"You haven't shown me any reason for answering them—like money?"

"All right," said Massey, "we're at the dickering stage anyway. Five hundred dollars for answering one of those questions—and it doesn't have to be the first one. Would you know Bill Quade if you saw him?"

"I'd like to see the five hundred dollars."

Pike Massey pulled out a desk drawer and produced four packets of bills, each packet with a band about it. He tossed one of the packets to Santa Fe Shaw.

Shaw took the packet and looked at the three remaining packets. "Yes," he said, "I'd know Bill Quade —if he was alive."

"Would you know him today—after not seeing him in ten years?"

"I said I'd know him."

Massey pushed the three packets of bills across the desk. "Will you earn the rest of this?"

Santa Fe Shaw looked at the money for a long

time. "Things have been mean lately. I've had a bad run of the cards and I could use two thousand dollars all right. I could use it like hell." He paused and continued to look at the money. "What was it that fellow Judas in the Bible got for selling out his friend?"

"Thirty pieces of silver."

"But he only betrayed his friend. He didn't have to kill him."

"Quade was your friend, then?"

Santa Fe Shaw shrugged. "You paid for that one. It doesn't make any difference really."

"Were you with him at the Weber massacre?"

"Massacre?" repeated Santa Fe Shaw. "I guess massacre's the right word, all right. But it wasn't like they say it was." He stopped, and his tone when he continued had a stronger timbre to it. "Mr. Pike Massey, I learned to read and write when I was a boy and I keep my eyes and ears open, which is probably the reason I'm still alive. I know who owns this town and the only reason I came here was because my name wasn't Shaw ten years ago and nobody can prove a goddam thing today. So—you wouldn't be trying to pull a fancy one on me, would you, Mr. Massey?"

"No," said Massey. "I was with the Jayhawkers myself during the war and we could have shot at each other a couple of times. That's water in the creek. I sent for you because you've got a talent for one thing. A man who calls himself Sam Parker, but who I've got reason to believe is Bill Quade, has been giving me trouble here. For certain reasons I can't handle the trouble myself and that's why I'm willing to pay you two thousand dollars to take care of it."

Santa Fe Shaw got to his feet. "I'll sleep on it, Massey."

"The hotel's usually full up," said Massey. "You probably can't get a room there, but there's a cot in my office in back of a saloon my deputy and I own. You can bunk down there."

A thin smile came over the gun fighter's mouth. "That the reason you want me to sleep there? Or is it because you want to keep me out of sight?"

Chapter Twenty-two

There were fifty or more leaderless men on the prairie near Lodge Pole. After what had happened to some of them the day before, the men would be confused, worried. Their loyalty to Jim Duke would hold them together, but Parker was Duke's representative and he alone could reassure them that they had not been forgotten.

Shortly after dawn Parker got his horse from the livery stable and rode out of Lodge Pole. He had not yet returned to town when the Kansas & Pacific train pulled into the depot shortly after eight o'clock.

Among the passengers were Cathy and Jim Duke. Parker would not have recognized Cathy at first sight. The girl who wore Levis and cowboy boots at home was now dressed in the height of fashion. She wore a traveling suit of green velvet which had a bustle in back and was tight-fitting enough to reveal the contours of her breasts. Her coiffured hair was topped by a hat that had cost forty dollars in New Orleans.

Cathy hated her clothes, but her father had insisted on them and Cathy endured. In fact she secretly hoped that Sam Parker would be aware of how womanly she looked.

Parker was not at the depot, however, for the simple reason that her father had neglected to telegraph him of his impending arrival. For that matter, Jim Duke did not know yet that the second trail herd had arrived in Lodge Pole.

The conductor piled a half-dozen pieces of luggage on the depot platform. "Leave 'em here," Duke said. "I'll have somebody from the hotel come and pick them up." He accosted the conductor. "Where's the best hotel in town?"

"The *only* hotel," replied the conductor, "is around the corner, halfway up the street."

Jim Duke had a heavy cane upon which he leaned his weight, but aside from a bit of stiffness in his right leg, he was able to walk well enough.

As he and Cathy walked to the hotel, Duke surveyed the new town. "The general's got himself a right smart piece of property here. It's a new town, a clean town." His eyes lit upon the marshal's office and jail across the street and Duke chuckled. "Got themselves a smart-looking jailhouse too." He shook his head. "Can't be as bad as Dodge, however. Last spring when I was there they had the randiest collection of gun-totin' marshals ever collected in one town."

"I've heard those stories from the hands," declared Cathy, "but I never believed a single one of them. This town doesn't look any different from our Texas towns except that the houses are made of lumber instead of adobe." Then she added as an afterthought, "I like the wooden houses better."

They had reached the hotel and now entered. Eve Prescott was behind the desk while the day clerk was getting his breakfast.

"Good morning," she greeted the new arrivals. "I do hope you're not expecting a room. We're entirely filled up."

"That's ridiculous," exclaimed Jim Duke. "My daughter and I've just arrived from Texas."

Eve exclaimed, "You—you're not Jim Duke?"

"Why not?" boomed Duke.

Eve's eyes went to Cathy. "And you're Cathy! You—" she frowned. "You're not at all like I expected you to be."

"Who told you about me?" asked Cathy eagerly.

"George Lam and, for that matter, Sam Parker."

"Parker's here?" cried Duke.

"He's been here for several days." Eve's eyes went to the key slot. "But he's not in the hotel right now. His key's here."

She turned, glanced at the door to the general's office. "Could you wait one moment, please. I think we can arrange for a room."

"There are two of us," cried Duke. "Two rooms!"

Eve flashed him a smile and crossed to the office door. She opened the door quickly, went through and closed the door.

"Father," she exclaimed to the general who was at his desk. "Jim Duke's arrived. He and his daughter."

"Be damned!" exclaimed General Prescott, getting quickly to his feet.

"They want rooms," said Eve, "and Miss Duke—Cathy—she's not at all what I expected. She's a real Southern lady—a belle."

"Good," said the general. "Maybe you and she can become friends." He stopped. "Play along, Eve—it's important." He crossed to the door, opened it and became the general of cavalry, meeting another general officer.

"Mr. Duke, may I welcome you to Kansas? I'm General Prescott."

When Parker returned to Lodge Pole at ten-thirty, Jim Duke and Cathy were already ensconced in two rooms at the hotel, the rooms having been provided for them by the simple expedient of evacuating the persons who had occupied them.

Parker dismounted in front of the hotel, rubbed his chin and debated whether to get a shave at the barber shop before or after having breakfast across the street. He decided to eat first and was about to start across the street when the clerk darted out of the hotel and called to him.

"Mr. Parker, the general's been asking about you. He'd like to talk to you as soon as possible."

"I'll see him after I have breakfast," said Parker.

"It's important. Your, ah, boss is with him. Mr. Duke."

"Here? Jim Duke's here?"

The clerk bobbed his head. "He's in the general's office."

Parker entered the hotel, went behind the desk and opened the door of the general's office. Duke saw him and sprang to his feet, wincing as he put his weight upon his recently broken leg.

'Parker!" he roared. "You're a sight for sore eyes." He grasped Parker's hand and pounded his back with his other hand. "The general and I were just talkin' about you."

"I'm glad you're here, Mr. Duke," began Parker.

"Mister Duke!" roared Duke. "You been away for a couple of weeks and now it's *Mister* Duke. Jim, boy, Jim and don't forget it. Take the weight off your feet and join us in a drink."

"It's too early in the morning for me," said Parker. "But I'd like to have a talk with you as soon as you're free."

"Of course, Parker, of course. And I want to ride out to the herd with you too." He suddenly scowled. "You know, of course, that I had to fire that damn fool Lam."

"He's dead," said Parker, "and so is Wes Conger. And Porfirio Pablos."

Jim Duke stared at Parker in utter amazement. "What's been goin' on here? Has the North declared war on us again?"

Parker looked at General Prescott. The general rose to the occasion. "You're an old trail hand, Duke. You've been to Abilene, Wichita and Dodge. You know what it's like, hot-blooded Texans, cold-blooded Yanks. They get together and there's trouble. I regret to say that we've had our share of it. But these things needn't concern you and me, Mr. Duke. We're business men. You're here to sell cattle. I'm here to buy them from you. We can discuss business amicably over a glass of whiskey."

Duke stared at the general, but his eyes kept going

back to the sober face of Sam Parker. He finally shook his head in bewilderment. "I'm sorry, General, what Parker's just told me has upset me greatly. I—you'll have to indulge me. We'll resume our discussions later. Right now I think I'd better have a little visit with my friend, Parker."

"Of course," said Prescott affably. "Have your talk, then we'll get together again. But let me assure you *again,* there's no cause for *us* to quarrel. No matter what you hear, we can come to an arrangement."

Jim Duke nodded absently. "Of course, General." He gripped Parker's arm hard and they left the general's office. Duke started for the stairs to go up to the second floor, then stopped. "Cathy's room is next door to mine. I think I'd rather talk to you alone first. Where can we go?"

Parker hesitated. "The restaurant across the street probably."

They left the hotel and started across the street, Duke shaking his head as he walked beside Parker. "Lam, Conger, Porfirio—that'll be hell breaking the news to his wife. She's got four children. Of course I'll take care of them. Still—Porfirio grew up on the ranch. His father went to work for *my* father."

"The worst mistake of your life," said Parker, "was that day in St. Louis when you asked me to come to Texas with you."

Duke stopped abruptly in the middle of the street. "What the hell are you talking about, Parker? That was the *best* thing I ever did. You've proved yourself. You took over when I couldn't and you brought the herd up here with about half the hands you should have had."

Parker shook his head. "I was the wrong man, at the wrong time."

"You've got to stop down-talking yourself, Parker."

"Parker," said Parker, "that was the first mistake. Parker's a name I've used for a good many years, but if I'd told you my real name there in St. Louis none of this would have happened."

"For Chrissake," cried Jim Duke. "We're back on

that subject. What's the big mystery about your real name? Go ahead, tell me and see if it makes any difference."

"My name," said Parker, "is Bill Quade."

For an instant the name made no impression on Jim Duke. Then he gasped, "Bloody Bill Quade, the guerrilla!"

"The bloodiest man of the war," said Parker, quoting. "The man who sacked Weber, Kansas, and murdered a hundred and twenty people."

"That's war-atrocity talk," snapped Duke. Then, "It really happened?"

"It happened," said Parker, "but not the way the newspapers said it did. I fought some Union soldiers near Weber and their casualties may have been a hundred and twenty men." He hesitated. "The commander of the Union cavalry was Major Prescott. He became a general later."

Duke gasped. "And he doesn't know you're Bill Quade?"

"Somebody's going to find out sooner or later. That's why I didn't want to come to Kansas."

"Sam!" shrieked a feminine voice from the direction of the hotel. "Sam Parker!"

"It's Cathy," exclaimed Jim Duke, then quickly, "not a word of this to her."

Parker stared in astonishment at the Cathy who was running toward them. He was totally unprepared for the way she looked in her feminine apparel—and he wasn't prepared for the way she met him. She came flying toward him, threw her arms about him and kissed him on the mouth. "Sam!" she babbled. "Sam Parker, you're the best thing I've seen since we left Texas."

"Cathy!" roared Jim Duke. "You're making a spectacle of yourself—in public!"

Cathy withdrew from Parker's arms, but gripped his hands and held them as she looked at him. "You're even handsomer than I remembered you," she said. "I'm *glad!*" She suddenly stepped away from him. "How do you like me in these—these *duds?*"

"They're very, ah, pretty," said Parker lamely.

"I'm going to take them off," declared Cathy. "I brought my regular clothes along and I'm going to put them on and get a horse and ride out to the herd with you. You *are* going out there, aren't you?"

"I've just come from there," said Parker. "The herd's all right." He looked at Jim Duke for help. "Your father and I have some things to discuss."

"Oh, business!" snorted Cathy. "You can talk that any time. In fact, since when do you have to talk business without me? I know every danged thing about Jim's business." She made a sudden moue. "It was me made him fire that danged George Lam—I'll tell him a thing or two when I see him." She saw the sudden twitch on Parker's face and became suspicious. "He's here, isn't he?"

"Later, Cathy," said Duke brusquely. "Go back to the hotel. I've got to talk to Parker alone—understand?"

"No, I don't understand," declared Cathy. "You're trying to evade me again. It's about George—something's happened to him."

"I'll talk to you about him later," said Duke, becoming angry. "I mean it, Cathy. Go to your room."

"Something's happened to George." She looked searchingly at Parker. "You had another fight with him." Her eyes fell suddenly to the gun that Parker was wearing. "You're wearing a gun. You—you killed him!"

"No," said Parker, "he *is* dead, but I—didn't kill him."

"Then who . . . ?"

Parker looked at Jim Duke. The cattleman groaned. "Dammit, Cathy, we can't stand here in the street all day discussing our troubles."

"What other troubles?"

"All hell's broke loose," snapped Jim Duke. "George is dead, Wes Conger's dead, Porfirio Pablos . . ."

"Oh, no!" wailed Cathy, tears suddenly streaming from her eyes. "I felt so good a minute ago and now . . ." She whirled suddenly and ran away from Parker and Duke, her hands covering her face.

Jim Duke swore roundly. "Isn't there *some* place we can be alone?"

Parker saw the new building up the street, the place where he had fought Pike Massey the day before.

"Yes," he said, "there's a vacant store. What you said to Cathy is true. All hell may break loose at any moment and I think you should have the full story before it happens. So you can act accordingly."

Chapter Twenty-three

Santa Fe Shaw slept until eleven o'clock, then the noise in The Kansas Saloon awakened him. He got up, went into the saloon and had a glass of whiskey at the bar. He put a bill on the bar, but the bartender shook his head. He had been told about the guest in the back room.

"No charge."

Santa Fe nodded carelessly, downed the whiskey and left the saloon. The bartender shook his head. He knew about Santa Fe Shaw.

Santa Fe found the restaurant, ordered a substantial breakfast and ate it slowly. When he came out of the restaurant he stood in front of it a moment, picking his teeth with a toothpick. He looked toward the jail, but was not yet ready to talk to Pike Massey.

His eyes fell upon two men coming along the wooden sidewalk from beyond the jail. The men were Jim Duke and Parker. Santa Fe's eyes were on Parker.

Parker did not see him, however, until he and Duke were within twenty feet of Santa Fe. Then Parker's eyes fell upon Santa Fe and he stopped.

His eyes still on Santa Fe Shaw, Parker said to Jim Duke, "I'll join you at the hotel, Jim."

"What the . . . ?" began Duke, then stopped. He followed Parker's eyes, picked out the object of his stare. "Someone you know?"

"Yes," said Parker quietly, "someone I haven't seen in a long time. If you don't mind . . ."

He walked away from Duke, going toward Santa Fe Shaw.

Santa Fe watched Parker approach. When Parker stopped before him he said, "Hiyah, Captain—long time . . ."

"Proxmire," Parker said.

Santa Fe Shaw chuckled. "Proxmire! I ain't used that name in a long time. It's Shaw now—Santa Fe Shaw they usually call me, because that's where I tell 'em I'm from. I've never been near the danged place." He shook his head. "I guess those reports about you been exaggerated a mite. You don't look dead at all."

"That would have been the easy way," said Parker heavily. "What have you been doing all these years?"

Santa Fe Shaw's face registered disappointment. "You mean you never heard of Santa Fe Shaw?"

"I'm afraid I haven't."

"Where you been, Captain? Hell, I'm famous." He chuckled again. "Remember, I used to be pretty handy with a Colt? Well, that's what I been doin'—using the Colt." He added flatly, "I'm a killer."

Parker stared at Santa Fe Shaw, who had once been a corporal under him when they had first organized as a quasi-military command. He said, "You kill people—for a living?"

"Sometimes I do it to keep the other fella from killin' me." He paused. "That's why I'm in this town. I was brung here to kill a man."

He saw the question in Parker's eyes and nodded. "You."

Parker shook his head slowly. "You'll have to get in line, Corporal. There are two or three people here ahead of you who want to kill me."

"Not bad enough to face you with a gun, Cap'n. That's why they sent for me."

"Am I supposed to guess who?"

"You don't have to. I'll tell you. Pike Massey. He paid me five hundred dollars to identify you. And he wants to give me fifteen hundred more to gun you down."

"You're going to do it?"

"What would you do you were in my place, Cap'n?"

"You're no longer in my command, Corporal. I can't think for you now. Whatever you decide, let me know."

"I ain't goin' to shoot you in the back. Never did that in my life, Cap'n. 'Less it was the goddam Yanks when they was runnin' from us. Like that time at Weber," he chuckled reminiscently. "We sure shot hell out of that bunch of scared rabbits!"

"They had a poor commander, Corporal." Parker jerked his thumb in the direction of the hotel. "Major Prescott, who became a general . . ."

Shaw nodded. "I know. Wouldn't his eyes bulge if you and me was to walk up to him and remind him of what we done to him in Weber?" He was still chuckling when Parker went off.

Parker was nearing the hotel when the general came storming out. He had a cigar stuck in his mouth and his face wore a scowl. He did not even look at Parker as he passed him.

Jim Duke had gone into the hotel, but when Parker reached the door he stopped to look back upon the street. The general was heading for the marshal's office.

Pike Massey was standing by the window. Long Jack was at the gunrack cleaning a Winchester repeating rifle. Massey had been at the window throughout the meeting of Parker and Santa Fe Shaw. He had noted the attitude of Santa Fe Shaw as he talked to his former commander, and he had not liked it.

The general slammed open the door of the office and came storming in. "Look here, Massey," he said angrily, "it's time me and you had a showdown."

"You're right, General," agreed Massey quite cheerfully.

Prescott was heedless of the presence of the tall deputy and the prisoners across the room behind the bars. "I know that you've sent for a killer to shoot down

Parker. I want you to go over to the telegraph office right now, this minute, and send a wire telling the man not to come."

"I can't do that," said Massey, glancing through the window and seeing Santa Fe Shaw, who still stood in front of the restaurant. "It's too late. The man's already here."

"Then run him out of town, or put him behind those bars. There's been enough killing in this town and I won't have any more. Not if I have to fire every one of you and close down this town to do it."

"Why, General," said Pike Massey mockingly, "I'm only doing you a favor by having Parker killed."

"I don't want that kind of favor. I mean that, Massey!"

"I think you'll change your mind," said Massey, "if I tell you Parker's real name. It's Bill Quade!"

General Prescott blinked twice, then shock struck him. His eyes popped wide open, his jaws fell agape and a violent shudder ran through him.

"Quade's dead!" he gasped.

Massey pointed through the window. "That's Santa Fe Shaw, the man I brought to town. I don't know his real name, but during the war he rode with Bloody Bill Quade." Massey's voice rang out suddenly. "He was with Quade at Weber, Kansas!"

The general almost reeled to the window. He peered through the unwashed window pane, looked long at Santa Fe Shaw. He did not recognize him, but there had been a note of certainty in Massey's voice and he knew that the marshal had spoken the truth.

He turned slowly and stared at Pike Massey.

"Parker is Bloody Bill Quade," Massey went on. "Shaw identified him. Now do you want Shaw to go through with it? Or do *you* want the satisfaction of personally killing Quade?"

The general seemed to age ten years. His shoulders drooped, his facial muscles became slack. Saliva dribbled from the corner of his mouth and his eyesight seemed to become dim. He peered up at Pike Massey.

Pike Massey said relentlessly, "He's got to be killed, General, doesn't he? 'Cause if he isn't he might tell the *real* story of what happened at Weber, Kansas!"

Soundlessly, General Prescott turned away from the marshal. He went to the door and went out. Massey watched him through the window, saw him reach the hotel, and then he drew a deep breath and went out of the office.

He walked casually toward Santa Fe Shaw. "The old feller who just left my office, that was General Prescott. Recognize him?"

Santa Fe Shaw shrugged. "His back looked mighty familiar. That's all I saw of him back there in Weber. He was runnin' like hell."

"You talked to Quade," prodded Massey, "and you've had your night to sleep on it."

Bucko Smith prevented Santa Fe Shaw from giving Massey his answer. He came charging out of a saloon waving a repeating rifle that he had appropriated somewhere. He was roaring drunk and wanted Lodge Pole and the world to know it.

"Yip-yip-yippee!" he howled. Then he pulled the trigger of the rifle. The gun boomed and its slug crashed the window of the restaurant before which Santa Fe Shaw and Pike Massey were standing.

Pike Massey had been a lawman too long to let such flagrant transgression go by. He wheeled, strode toward Bucko Smith.

"Throw down that gun," he cried, "throw it down, or by God I'll bend this Colt over your head."

"You and who else?" roared Bucko Smith. Then he recognized Massey. "Hey—it's the marshal—the fella I told about Bill Quade." He blinked owlishly, peered around past Massey in the general direction of the jail from which Long Jack was just emerging.

"Where is he?" Bucko Smith howled. "The big bad guerrilla who whupped the hell out of you Yankees. Hey—Bloody Bill! Bloody Bill Quade, come on and let me show these damn Yankees how we treat tough guys like you down in Louisiana. C'mon, Bloody Bill Quade! Show yourself."

"Damn you," snarled Pike Massey, lunging toward the former prison camp overseer. He whipped out his revolver, swung it at Smith's head.

The only thing that saved Bucko Smith was the rifle. He had levered a fresh cartridge into the chamber and was swinging the rifle around just as Massey struck at him. The Colt banged against the barrel, but the force of the blow behind it caused Smith's finger, already on the trigger, to pull on it.

The bullet went across the street, through the front window of the Prescott Hotel. It missed Sam Parker by a good three feet, but it struck the day clerk in the face. The man cried out and fell down behind the desk.

The voice of Bucko Smith rolled across the street into the hotel. "Hey, Bill Quade—Sam Parker, come on out. Lemme show these Yanks how I used to flog you down in Louisiana."

A Colt barked spitefully and Bucko Smith's challenge was cut short.

Bucko Smith stood swaying, staring unbelievingly at Pike Massey, who had just shot him. "Be goddamned," he whispered, "be goddamned."

He crumpled to his knees, then fell forward onto his face.

Parker stepped out of the hotel. He started across the street. Long Jack was the first to see him. He stopped abruptly a dozen feet from Pike Massey, faced the oncoming Parker. Pike Massey, his revolver already in his hand, turned, saw Parker coming toward him. He let the Colt dangle muzzle downward.

Behind him Arch Bender appeared in the doorway of the restaurant.

Parker came steadily across the street. Massey threw down the gauntlet. "You heard the man," he said. "He named you—Bill Quade, Bloody Bill Quade."

Parker stopped. He was twenty feet from Massey, about the same distance from Long Jack. Arch Bender was behind Massey a dozen feet. And a few feet to the right of Massey was Santa Fe Shaw.

Parker's eyes went from Massey to Long Jack, to Arch Bender and finally to Santa Fe Shaw.

Frank Gruber

"Well, Corporal," Parker said, "what's it going to be?"

"Earn your money!" snarled Massey, gesturing to Santa Fe Shaw.

Santa Fe Shaw reached deliberately under his coat and brought out a packet of greenbacks. He threw the money at Massey's feet. "This money's no good, Massey. It's got to be silver—thirty pieces." A cheerful smile came over his features.

"All right, *Captain!*"

It was Arch Bender who fired the first shot. He was on the doorstep behind Massey and could see over the marshal's head. His hand whipped down to his holster, came up with the revolver in his fist. It roared and a bullet tore through the flesh of Parker's left thigh.

Parker threw himself forward to the ground, drawing the gun in his holster at the same time. He was very slow on the draw; it was something that required a great deal of practice which he had not had.

Pike Massey's bullet, fired from the gun already in the clear, went through his back, missing his spine by less than an inch. Massey died the instant after he had pulled the trigger. Santa Fe Shaw's bullet crashed through his brain. Shaw did not even wait to see the result of his shot. He wheeled in the same motion, fired at Arch Bender.

The deputy cried out, staggered and Shaw's second bullet, going through his throat, silenced him forever. As badly wounded as he was, Parker managed to raise the muzzle of his revolver. He sighted along it, gasped as Long Jack's bullet went through his shoulder—and then pulled the trigger.

The bullet went true. The fight was over. The three marshals were dead, Parker was seriously wounded but Santa Fe Shaw was without a scratch, although he had killed two of the three dead men.

Chapter Twenty-four

       Parker, who had once been known as Bill Quade, was unconscious for almost twenty-four hours and for another two days he hovered between life and death.

The single doctor in Lodge Pole extracted the three slugs from his body, shaking his head over and over as he encountered the myriad scars on the lean body.

"He's tough," he told Jim Duke. "I wouldn't give an ordinary man one chance in a hundred, but this man, well, he just might make it."

On the third day Quade opened his eyes. The fever had gone down in his body, his eyes were bright. Cathy Duke, who sat on the chair beside his bed in the hotel, jumped to her feet, ran to the door and whipped it open.

"Jim!" she cried down the hotel corridor. "He's come around. Hurry!"

Then she turned back to Parker. She stood beside the bed, looked down at him and smiled. "Well, Bill Quade," she said, "I guess you're going to make it, after all."

"Why not?" asked Sam Parker—Bill Quade. "I've always made it before."

Jim Duke's heavy step was heard in the hall and then he came into the room, almost filling it with his huge presence. He stepped up to the bed, caught up the

151

right hand of Parker and squeezed it. "All right, feller," he boomed. "You ain't the most popular man in Kansas and it's time we got to hell and gone back to Texas."

"He won't be able to travel for weeks," cried Cathy Duke. "You know that. Besides, there's no hurry at all, now that the general's . . ."

She stopped. Duke chuckled hugely. "Now that the general's gone. Yep, kit and kaboodle. He's giving Lodge Pole back to the Indians."

"The herd," said Parker. "Did he buy it?"

"Hell, no," replied Jim Duke. "I wouldn't sell it to him. I'd rather let the cattle starve than do business with a man like the departed General Prescott."

"The herd's sold," said Cathy. "He's dying to tell you. He got twenty dollars a head."

"Not bad," chuckled Duke, "not bad for this time of the year." He winked at Parker. "With Prescott gone, the commission men formed their selves a little pool and bought their selves a mess of beef—all thirteen thousand head! I'm loaded with money, Parker, so do like Cathy said—get out of that bed and help me carry the green stuff back to Texas."

He caught Cathy's eyes, hesitated. "It's time for my afternoon glass of milk." He winked, went out of the room and closed the door.

"And you, Sam Parker," said Cathy sternly, "get back to sleep. You need a lot of it."

"I'm a little tired," admitted Parker, "but I want to know one thing more. Did—did Eve Prescott go with her father?"

"Of course," said Cathy. "She couldn't stand the competition." Cathy leaned over the bed and kissed Parker. She held her lips on his mouth for a long moment. Then raising her face an inch or two, she added, "This competition."

ABOUT THE AUTHOR

FRANK GRUBER started his career as a trade journal editor in the Midwest. Despite his success as one of the most prolific western writers in the world, Mr. Gruber always had a desire to follow a more journalistic career. He was the author of at least fifty books, more than fifty-four motion pictures, at least 350 magazine stories and dozens of television scripts. He created numerous western television serials, notably *Wells Fargo*, and was also known as a mystery writer.